Elsie and
Her Namesakes

The Original Elsie Classics

Elsie Dinsmore

Elsie's Holidays at Roselands

Elsie's Girlhood

Elsie's Womanhood

Elsie's Motherhood

Elsie's Children

Elsie's Widowhood

Grandmother Elsie

Elsie's New Relations

Elsie at Nantucket

The Two Elsies

Elsie's Kith and Kin

Elsie's Friends at Woodburn

Christmas with Grandma Elsie

Elsie and the Raymonds

Elsie Yachting with the Raymonds

Elsie's Vacation

Elsie at Viamede

Elsie at Ion

Elsie at the World's Fair

Elsie's Journey on Inland Waters

Elsie at Home

Elsie on the Hudson

Elsie in the South

Elsie's Young Folks

Elsie's Winter Trip

Elsie and Her Loved Ones

Elsie and Her Namesakes

Elsie and
Her Namesakes

Book Twenty-Eight of
The Original Elsie Classics

Martha Finley

CUMBERLAND HOUSE
NASHVILLE, TENNESSEE

Elsie and Her Namesakes
by Martha Finley

Any unique characteristics of this edition:
Copyright © 2001 by Cumberland House Publishing, Inc.

Published by Cumberland House Publishing, Inc.,
431 Harding Industrial Drive, Nashville, Tennessee 37211.

Cover design by Bruce Gore, Gore Studios, Inc.
Photography by Dean Dixon Photography
Hair and Makeup by Calene Rader
Text design by Heather Armstrong

Printed in the United States of America
1 2 3 4 5 6 7 8 — 05 04 03 02 01

Elsie and
Her Namesakes

CHAPTER FIRST

THINGS WERE GOING on quite blithely at Woodburn, as everybody was very deeply interested in the preparations for the quickly approaching wedding—including all the relatives and connections on the neighboring estates and those on more southern plantations. Woodburn seemed the center of attraction. Relatives and friends were constantly coming and going, and many consultations were held as to suitable gifts, especially for Gracie and Harold. There was great interest shown by all in the preparation of the trousseau, and Alma and one or two assistants were very busy with it.

There were many shopping expeditions, in which Gracie sometimes shared, though rather against Harold's wishes, so fearful was he that she might take cold or suffer from overexertion. He had long been her careful physician, but now he was not only that but also her promised husband. To please him, Gracie left the greater part of the shopping to the other members of the family and made some of her selections by samples brought by them or the mails.

In the meantime, plans for both the wedding ceremony and the honeymoon were discussed. Someone spoke of a trip to the North, but Harold vetoed that promptly. "It will be too late in the season now for Gracie to try that. I must take her to a warmer climate."

"Then let us all go to Viamede for the winter," suggested his mother. "Would that not suit you, Gracie dear?"

"Yes, indeed, Grandma Elsie. I think there is no sweeter spot upon earth for a warm winter holiday," was the pleased response.

"Then that is where we will go," Harold said with a happy laugh, "and I hope our mother and other dear ones will either accompany or follow us down there."

"Oh, I like that plan," exclaimed Violet, "but I think few of us will be quite ready to leave our homes here by the time the bridal party starts."

"Then suppose you go in relays," suggested Chester pleasantly.

"Why not say we, instead of you, brother Chester," laughed Elsie Raymond. "I'm sure grandma included you in her invitation."

"Certainly," said Grandma Elsie, giving Chester one of her sweet smiles. "May I not count you and Lucilla among my grandchildren?"

"Indeed, I am delighted to have you do so and proud to be able to claim a relationship," returned Chester. "But for the claims of business, I should be glad to accept your kind invitation. Those, however, will not permit it."

There were exclamations of regret from several of those present, Grandma Elsie among them.

"But Lu can go. Can't she, Chester?" asked Elsie Raymond.

"Go and leave my husband!" exclaimed Lucilla in mock indignation. "Who could suspect me of being so unfeeling a wife?"

"Oh, no, Lu, I didn't mean that," Elsie hastened to say. "I know you and Brother Chester are very fond of each other, but so are you and papa. And all the rest of us love you dearly, and we won't any of us like to do without you, even for a few weeks. Oh, Brother Chester, can't you get somebody else to manage your business while you go along with us?"

"No, little sister, and seeing my wife does not want to leave me, I am not willing to do without her, either."

"And you are quite right about it, Chester," said the captain, sighing slightly and giving his eldest daughter a look of warm, fatherly affection. "Much as I shall certainly miss her—even for the few weeks of our separation—I must concede that she is right in putting your claim to her companionship first."

"And I know it's right when you say so, papa. So, I'll try to be content," said Elsie cheerfully. "But both you and baby Mary will go with us. Won't you, Eva?"

"And leave Lu alone all day while Chester is away at his office? Oh, I couldn't think of doing that! And, besides, I think home is the best place for baby and me for the present," returned Evelyn, gazing lovingly down at the cooing babe upon her knee.

"Oh, thank you, Eva," cried Lucilla, clapping her hands in delight. "The thought of having you and baby left half reconciles me to seeing the others go, leaving me behind. Only—oh, father," with a pathetic look at him and a quiver of pain in her voice, "what shall I—what can I ever do without you?"

At that, he stepped to her side and laid his hand tenderly on her head.

"We will comfort ourselves with the thought that the parting will be for a brief season, daughter dear," he said in moved tones, "and with the prospect of the joyful reunion in store for us all in the spring."

"And you will help me with frequent letters, papa, dear. Won't you?" she asked, trying to speak lightly and cheerfully.

"I think there will be a daily bulletin, perhaps more than one—at least with Eva's share counted in," the captain replied with an affectionate look at his daughter-in-law and her babe.

"Oh, I hope so, father. Of course, Lu will share with me the pleasure of mine," responded Evelyn with a bright, glad look up into his eyes.

"And though Viamede is ever so delightful, I think we will all soon be in haste to get home to see our dear little baby girl," Elsie exclaimed, quickly hurrying to Eva's side to caress the little one asleep on her lap.

"Yes. We will all sadly miss both her and her mother," said Violet.

"Indeed we will," added her mother, "and I sincerely wish we could take her and all the Sunnyside folk with us. We will hope to do so the next time we go to Viamede."

This was an afternoon chat in the library, where they had gathered for the time. Some of the cousins were with them, and little, feeble Ned had been asleep on the couch.

"Go to Viamede? When will we go?" he asked feebly, rousing from his slumber just in time to catch his grandmother's concluding words.

"We hope to do so on the afternoon of the wedding day, carrying my pet patient along," replied Harold, taking the small, white hand in his and patting it affectionately.

"Papa and mamma, too?" queried Ned, rather anxiously, looking from one to the other.

"We are going in your papa's yacht, and they are to follow us in few days by rail and join us on the Florida coast. From there, we expect to go on together to Viamede."

"Oh, that's nice—but—oh, what will I do without papa and mamma? Will you and Gracie take care of me?"

"Some of the time, I think, but your grandma still more, your sister Elsie, and some of the cousins who will be with us, too will help to entertain you."

"And with all those, you can do without papa and mamma for a few days. Can't you, sonny boy?" queried Violet, leaning over him and softly patting his cheek caressingly.

"Yes, mamma. I love my dear grandma and uncle and Elsie—the cousins, too—but I'll miss you and papa."

"Then you must try to be patient and happy thinking it will be only a few days before we may hope to be together again," returned his mother, repeating her caresses.

"And you'll show yourself to be a manly little man of whom we can all be proud as well as fond," added his father, standing by his side, smoothing his hair and looking down smilingly into his face.

"I'll try, papa," responded the little fellow, "and I do believe we will have a nice time if—if I can keep on getting well."

"We will hope for that, and you will have your good doctor with you. And you must keep up your spirits with the thought that we expect to be all together again in a few days."

Grandma Elsie had been taking part in some of the business visits to the neighboring city, but now she decided to leave all that to the younger ladies and devote herself to the entertainment of Ned, Elsie, and others of the young people of the family connection who might care to share with them in listening to the interesting facts and stories that she would relate for Ned's enjoyment and instruction. She presently announced this determination, which was gladly received by all the children present, and asked if any of them could suggest a subject for tomorrow's discourse. Elsie responded with an eager look of delight and entreaty.

"Well, dear child, what is it?" asked her grandma.

"Something about Washington, grandma, beginning with what he did when he was a very young man. I'd like to hear all you can tell us about Braddock's defeat."

"Then that shall be our subject tomorrow, if all my audience should be pleased to have it so," was the kindly reply, to which several young voices responded with expressions of pleasure in the prospect.

CHAPTER SECOND

THE NEXT DAY, Grandma Elsie, remaining true to her promise, stayed at Woodburn, while the younger ladies went on their shopping expedition to the city. Ned had been carried down to the library and lay there on a sofa, his pale face bright with expectation, for he dearly loved grandma's stories, especially now when it seemed too great an exertion to hold a book and read for himself. His sister Elsie was there, too, and so were several of the young cousins from Ion and Fairview, who had come riding in on their bicycles full of joyful expectation, for their grandma's stories were to them a great delight.

They gathered about her, and she began.

"I am going to tell you of our Washington and some of his deeds and experiences. He has been called the Father of his Country. Someone once gave the toast, 'Washington: Providence left him childless that his country might call him father.'"

"Had he never any children at all, grandma?" asked Ned.

"None of his very own, but he had some stepchildren. He married a widow who had two children by a former husband.

"Washington was very young when he left school and began life as a surveyor. At sixteen, he was public surveyor of Culpeper County, and he continued there at that work for three years. Then, at nineteen, he was made adjutant-general with the rank of major in one of the four military districts into which Virginia was divided.

"In 1753, Great Britain instructed her governors in the American colonies to serve notice on the French that their forts built on western lands claimed by the English were an encroachment on her colonies. If the French resisted, they were instructed to use force to drive them away.

"Washington was then twenty-one—a tall, grave, handsome young man, and one with the talents and information required. He had courage, experience in the woods, knowledge about forts, and tact with the Indians. The governor offered the dangerous and difficult mission to him, and he accepted it.

"This was in the summer. In October, the governor resolved to enlarge his army to ten companies of one hundred men each, but no officer in that Virginia regiment was to rank higher than captain. Indignant at that, Washington resigned and left the army.

"The next February, Braddock came from England with two regiments of troops, supplies, and artillery. He landed in Virginia, and Washington sent him a congratulatory letter. Shortly afterward, Braddock invited him to become his aide-de-camp, and he willingly accepted the invitation. He joined Braddock at Frederickstown, feeling much displeased that the army should pass through Maryland instead of Virginia.

"Braddock—proud Englishman—despised all colonials except Franklin and Washington, but from the beginning he was pleased with those two gentlemen."

"Colonial, grandma?" said Ned, inquiringly.

"Yes, dear. You must remember that at that time there was no United States of America. Instead, there were just thirteen colonies subject to Great Britain, and they were all on or near the Atlantic coast. Our country has grown very much since then."

"In more ways than one. Hasn't it, grandma?" remarked Elsie Raymond with a look of pride.

"Yes, dear, it is many times as large and as wealthy and full of comforts and conveniences. Indeed, I think we may safely say that we are the richest and most powerful nation of the world. God has been wonderfully good to us, and to Him be all the glory and praise.

"In the days I am telling you of there were no railroads, and the rough mountain roads would be very difficult to cross with the heavy artillery and baggage. Therefore, Washington urged a forward movement with a small but chosen band and only such artillery and light stores as were absolutely necessary.

"Washington went with the rear division, riding in a covered wagon, for he had been quite sick with a fever and pains in his head and was not yet able to sit a horse. He overtook the advance division at the mouth of the Youghiogheny River fifteen miles from Fort Duquesne, and the next morning, though still very weak in body, he attended Braddock on horseback. The ground was very steep on the north side of the Monongahela, which made it necessary to ford the river twice and march a part of the way on the south side. About noon, they were within ten miles of Fort Duquesne. It was here they crossed to the north side, and their road lay through a level plain at the north end of which a gradual ascent began, leading to hills of some height and then through an uneven country covered with trees. Three hundred men under Colonel Gage marched first, then came another party of two hundred, then Braddock came with the main body, artillery, and baggage.

"All had crossed the river, and the advance body was going cheerfully up the hill, on each side of which was a ravine eight or ten feet deep covered with trees and long grass. General Braddock had not employed any scouts. He despised Indians, colonists, and their irregular kind of warfare. A hundred friendly Indians had joined him on the march, but he treated them so coldly, in spite of all Washington could say in their favor, that they had all gone away. They came again on the very night before this dress parade between the ravines, and again they offered their assistance. But in spite of all

Washington could say in favor of employing them, the general refused to do so."

"And were the French and their Indians hiding in those ravines, grandma?" asked Ned.

"Yes," she replied. "That was just what they were doing, and after the first British division had gotten well into the field between the ravines without seeing or hearing an enemy, they suddenly received a volley of musket balls in their faces. As one of the soldiers afterward said, they could only tell where the enemy were hiding by the smoke of their muskets. The British at once returned a fire that killed the French commander, and it was so heavy that the Indians thought it came from artillery. They were about to retreat when Dumas, who was in command now that his superior officer was killed, rallied them and sent them under French officers to attack the right flank while he held the front.

"The British now received another furious rain of bullets, and the woods rang with the savage yells of the Indians, but they could see only smoke, except when now and then an Indian ventured from behind a tree to take a scalp. The Virginians, used to the Indians' way of fighting, dropped to the ground or rushed behind trees, and the British regulars tried to imitate them. Braddock, just then reaching the scene, was furious at that. Riding about the field, he forced his men, both British and Virginians, back into the ranks, just where the enemy could get full sight of them and shoot them down more readily."

"Why, grandma, what did he do that for?"

"It seems he wanted them to keep rank just because he considered that the right thing to do."

"Stupid old fellow!" exclaimed on the other young listeners.

"Yes, he does not seem to have been very bright in that particular line," assented Mrs. Travilla, "but he was very brave. Four horses were shot out from under him, and he mounted a fifth. All his aides had been shot down but one—our Washington. Though he was hardly well enough to sit in his saddle, he rode about the field delivering Braddock's orders to the troops, so making himself a conspicuous target for the enemy, who fired at him again and again. But they could not kill him—did not even succeed in wounding him, though two horses were shot from under him. He sprang upon a third and went fearlessly on with his work."

"But he was not wounded. I remember reading that," said Elsie. "Surely, grandma, God took care of him that he might after a while become the father of this country."

"Yes, God protected him, and that made it impossible for the foe to destroy him."

"But the French killed Braddock. Didn't they?" asked Ned.

"We really don't know," replied Mrs. Travilla. "Braddock was fatally wounded at that time, but I have seen an account of his fatal wounding, which may or not be true. It is thought that among the Americans who were in the fight were two of the name of Fausett—brothers named Thomas and Joseph. Thomas is said to have been a man of gigantic frame and of uncivilized propensities. It is said that he spent most of his life in the mountains, living as a hermit on the game that he killed. In the battle we are talking of, he saw his brother behind a tree and saw Braddock ride up to him in a passion and strike him down with his sword. Tom Fausett drew up his rifle instantly and shot Braddock through the lungs, partly in revenge for the outrage upon his brother and partly, as he always declared, to get the general out of the way so that he might sacrifice no more of the lives of the British and Americans."

"Why, grandma, did he want his own men killed?" asked Ned.

"No, but he was foolish, obstinate, and totally determined to have his own way. Those who appointed him commander of that force made a great mistake. He was a good tactician, but he was proud, prejudiced, and conceited. Talking with Benjamin Franklin, who was then the postmaster-general, he said, 'After taking Fort Duquesne, I am to proceed to Niagara, and having taken that, to Frontenac, if the season will allow time, and I suppose it will, for Duquesne can hardly detain me above three or four days. Then I can see nothing that can obstruct my march to Niagara.' Franklin thought the plan excellent if he could see his fine troops safely to Fort Duquesne, but he told him there might be danger from Indian ambuscades. The savages, shooting unexpectedly from their places of concealment in the woods, might destroy his army in detail. Braddock thought that an absurd idea and replied that the Indians might be formidable enemies to raw American troops, but it was impossible they should make an impression upon the King's regular and disciplined troops. And, as I have already told you, that was the idea that he acted upon in the fight, which is always spoken of as 'Braddock's defeat.' He insisted that his men should be formed in regular platoons. They fired by platoons—at the rocks into the bushes and ravines—and so killed not enemies only, but many Americans, as many as fifty by one volley."

"Oh, how dreadful!" cried Elsie, "killing their own comrades instead of the enemies they were fighting with."

"Grandma, did Tom Fausett's shot kill Braddock at once?" asked Ned.

"No. It was on the ninth of July he was shot, and he died on the evening of the thirteenth. It was on that day that the remnant of his army went into camp at the Great Meadows. In the evening after the fight, Braddock exclaimed, 'Who would have thought it?'

"Then he remained silent until a few minutes before he died, when he said, 'We should better know how to deal with them another time.' They buried him before daybreak in the road and leveled his grave with the ground, lest the Indians should find and mutilate his body. The chaplain had been wounded, and Washington read the burial service."

"At the Great Meadows, grandma?" asked Elsie Raymond.

"About a mile from Fort Necessity," replied Mrs. Travilla. "I have read that on the seventeenth, the sick and wounded reached Fort Cumberland. The next day Washington wrote to a friend that since his arrival there he had heard a circumstantial account of his own death and dying speech. Now he was taking the earliest opportunity of contradicting the first and of giving the assurance that he had not yet composed the latter."

"Well, I hope he got the praise he deserved from somebody," said Elsie.

"Yes, he did," replied her grandma. "A very eloquent and accomplished preacher, a Reverend Samuel Davies, who a few years after became president of Princeton College, did so in a sermon to one of the companies organized after Braddock's defeat. After praising the zeal and courage of the Virginia troops, he added: 'As a remarkable instance of this, I may point out to the public that heroic youth, Colonel Washington, whom I cannot but hope Providence has hitherto preserved in so signal a manner for some important service to his country.'"

"And doesn't it seem that that was what God preserved him for, grandma?" exclaimed Elsie, her eyes shining with pleasure.

"It does, indeed. God was very good to us in giving us such a leader for such a time as that of our hard struggle for the freedom that had made us the great and powerful nation that we now are."

"And we are not the only people that think very highly of Washington," remarked one of the cousins.

"No, indeed," replied Mrs. Travilla. "One English historian has said that Washington's place in the history of mankind is without a fellow, and Lord Brougham said more than once, 'It will be the duty of the historian in all ages to let no occasion pass of commemorating this illustrious man. Until time shall be no more will a test of the progress which our race has made in wisdom and virtue be derived from the veneration paid to the immortal name of Washington.'"

"That's high praise, grandma. Isn't it?" asked Eric Leland. "I think our Washington deserved every word of it."

"As do I," she replied. "He was just, generous, disinterested—spending so many of the best years of his life in fighting for the freedom of his country and that without a cent of pay. He was wise, fearless, heroic, self-sacrificing. He feared God, believed in Christ, was a man of prayer, fully acknowledging divine aid and direction in all that he attempted and all he accomplished. He was a wonderful man—truly a God-given leader to us in a time when such an one as he was very sorely needed."

"When was the war quite over, grandma?" asked Ned.

"The treaty of peace was signed in Paris on the twentieth of January in 1783," replied Mrs. Travilla. "News did not fly nearly so fast as it does now, and it was not till the seventeenth of the following April that Washington received the proclamation of peace by our Congress. On the nineteenth of April on the anniversary of the shedding of the first blood of the war at Lexington eight years before, the cessation was proclaimed at the head of every regiment of the army. That was by Washington's general orders, in which he added: 'The chaplains of the several brigades will render thanks to Almighty God for all His mercies, particularly for His overruling the wrath of man to His own glory, and causing the rage of war to cease among the nations.'"

CHAPTER THIRD

NOTICING NOW THAT weak little Ned began to look weary and sleepy, Mrs. Travilla bade the other children go out and amuse themselves a while wherever they liked about the house and grounds. So they quietly left the room.

"Please, don't go away, grandma. Please stay beside me while I take my nap," murmured the little fellow, opening his eyes to look up at her and closing them again.

"No, darling, I won't," she said soothingly. "I have a book and am going to sit here beside you and read while you sleep."

Elsie and the others refreshed themselves with some lively sport upon the lawn. Then the young guests, thinking it time to return to their homes, mounted their bicycles and departed, leaving Elsie sitting in the veranda, whiling away the time with a bit of fancy work while waiting and watching for the return of father and mother and the other loved ones from their city shopping.

Meantime, she was thinking how very much she would like to give her dear sister Gracie a handsome wedding present and regretting that she had not expected the wedding to come so soon and saved her pocket money for that very purpose. She had not wasted it, but she had been more liberal in gifts to some others and spent more in self-indulgences than now seemed to have been at all necessary.

But these regretful meditations were at length interrupted by the carriage turning in at the great gates and coming swiftly up the driveway.

"Oh, I am so glad that you have come back at last, papa, mamma, and all the rest of you dear folks," she exclaimed, hastening to meet them as they alighted and came up the veranda steps. "I suppose you have bought ever so many beautiful things."

"Yes, we have," replied her mother.

"Many more than were at all necessary," laughed Gracie. "If this sort of kindness killed, I am afraid I should not live very long."

"But it does not, and you look very rosy and well for you," laughed Elsie as Gracie reached her side, put an arm about her, and gave her a fond kiss.

"Yes, she stood the ordeal very well so far," remarked Dr. Harold, giving his affianced a very lover-like glance and smile.

"I am ever so glad of that," said Elsie. "Oh, I do want to see all those pretty things you purchased! Mayn't they be carried into the library, mamma? Grandma and Ned will want to see them, and they are in there."

"Yes," replied Violet, leading the way, "and we will all go in there and examine them together. I hear Ned talking, so there is no danger of waking him out of a nap."

All followed her lead, a servant bearing the heavier packages, bringing up the rear. All enjoyed examining the purchases—rich silks, laces, ribbons, and jewelry—and some minutes were spent in lively chat over them and about other pretty things seen in the city stores.

Then Gracie was summoned to the sewing room to inspect the work going on there. Violet went with her, and Harold hastened away to see a patient, the captain and Elsie following him as far as the veranda. When Harold had gone, the captain seated himself and drew Elsie to his knee, as was his wont when they had a moment to sit still and chat together.

"Well, my darling little daughter," he said, "I hope you have had a pleasant time at home with grandma and Ned and your cousins while papa and mamma were away?"

"Yes, sir. Grandma was telling us about Braddock's defeat, and it was very interesting. So the time passed very pleasantly. Papa, what beautiful things you and mamma and the rest brought home from the city! I wish," she paused, blushing and hanging her head.

"Well, dear child, speak out and tell papa what you want," he said encouragingly.

"I was just wishing I could buy a handsome wedding gift for dear Gracie, but I did not think she was going to be married so soon, and—and my pocket money is almost all gone."

"Well, never mind," he said with a smile and patting her cheek. "I have been considering an increase in your pocket money for you and Ned just at this time. I shall give each of you fifty dollars tomorrow to do with exactly as you please—buy for yourselves or for others or save up for some future time."

"Oh, papa, thank you, thank you!" she cried joyously. "And now can you tell me what to buy for Gracie and Harold?"

"We will consult mamma about that," he said, "and perhaps she will go with us into the city tomorrow to make the purchase."

"Ah, Elsie wanting to do some shopping, too?" asked Violet's pleasant voice as she stepped out from the hall door to the veranda and came quickly toward them. "No," she said to her husband, "do not get up. I will take a seat by your side," suiting the action to the word.

"Yes, mamma," answered the little girl. "Surely I ought to give a wedding present to sister Gracie, and papa is going to give me money—fifty dollars—to buy it with."

"Oh, that is nice," said Violet. "Levis, my dear, you are certainly the best of fathers, as well as of husbands. Do you know that?"

"According to my very partial wife," he returned with a pleased little laugh.

"And this one of your daughters, too, papa," said Elsie.

"As well as every member of the kith and kin who know him well," added Violet. "What are you thinking of buying with that large sum of money, Elsie?"

"I want your advice about that, mamma."

"I believe Gracie feels very rich now—in silks, satins, laces, and jewelry," Violet responded in a musing tone. "Ah, well, of that last, few ladies can have too much. A ring or a bracelet would hardly come amiss."

"No, mamma, I do not believe they would, and they would be becoming to sister's beautiful hands and arms. I wonder if Ned would not like to buy one or the other for her with his fifty dollars."

"Let us go to the library now and consult him about it," said the captain, setting Elsie down and rising to his feet as he spoke.

"The best plan, I think," said Violet. "He is sure to want to spend your gift to him in something for Gracie."

They found Ned still awake and pleased at their coming.

"You may be news-teller and questioner, Elsie," said their father, and she told her brother in hurried, joyous fashion what their father had promised and what she thought of buying for Gracie with her fifty dollars, concluding with the query, "What will you do with your fifty, Ned?"

"I do not know. I cannot go to the stores to find anything," he sighed disconsolately.

"But you can trust mamma and the rest of us to select something for you," suggested his father in tender tones.

"Oh, I guess that will do," responded Ned more cheerfully. "To be sure, I want it to be something handsome, if it costs every cent of the fifty dollars."

So that matter was settled, and the very next morning the captain, Violet, and Elsie drove into the city, visited the best jewelry store, and selected a beautiful ring and matching bracelet for Gracie. Elsie was so charmed with them that she seemed hardly able to think of anything else on the homeward drive.

"I hope Ned will be pleased with the bracelet," she said, "but if he would rather have the ring for his gift to Gracie, he may, and I will give the bracelet to her."

"That is right, daughter," said the captain. "I think they are both beautiful, and they cost very nearly the same."

They found Ned wide awake and full of eager expectation. He heard the carriage wheels on the driveway and cried out, "There they are, grandma, and oh, how I wish I could run out to the veranda to meet them!"

"Never mind about that, sonny boy. They will be in here directly," was the kind response, and the next minute Elsie came running in, holding up two little parcels.

"We have bought them, Ned," she cried. "They are just lovely, and you may open the packages and take your choice which one to have for your gift to Gracie," and she put them in his hands as she spoke.

He looked delighted, hastily tore open the larger package, and cried out, "Oh, I will take this for mine. It is the prettiest bracelet I ever saw!"

"But the ring is every bit as beautiful," said Elsie, "and I do not care in the least which you give and which will be my present to Gracie."

"And since you do not care in the least, it won't matter who gives which," laughed their mother.

"And that makes it easy for you both," said the captain, drawing up a chair to the side of the couch for his wife and seating himself close by her side.

"What do you think of them, mother?" turning to Grandma Elsie.

"That they are both beautiful," she replied. "Gracie is sure to be greatly pleased with them. Ah, here she comes!" as the young girl came in followed by Harold.

"Oh, Gracie, here are our wedding gifts to you—Elsie's and mine. Come look at them," cried Ned, raising himself to a sitting posture in his excitement.

"Oh, they are lovely, lovely!" she responded, taking them from his hands, turning them about in hers, and gazing upon them delightedly. "But," she added in a regretful tone, "I am afraid you have both spent far too much on me."

"Not at all, daughter. They were bought with both your mamma's and my full approval," said the captain. "What do you think of them, Harold?" as he, too, seemed to be giving the trinkets a critical examination.

"I entirely agree in the opinion Gracie has just expressed," he replied. "They are quite worthy of the admiration of us all. Must have cost a pretty penny, I should say."

"But not too much for gifts to our dear sister Gracie," said Elsie.

"No, no. I quite agree with you in that opinion," replied Harold with a smile and a look of ardent love and admiration at the sweet face of his betrothed.

"Put them on, Gracie, and let us see how they look on your pretty hand and arm," pleaded Ned, and she complied.

"Ah, they fit nicely," she said with a pleased little laugh. She then took them off and replaced them in their boxes, adding, "They are far too handsome and costly to wear just now. They should be shown first along with the other Christmas and wedding gifts."

"Such a long, long time to wait," sighed Ned quite disconsolately.

"Not so very, Neddie boy," returned Grandma Elsie in her cheery tone. "This is Friday, and Christmas comes next week on Wednesday."

"Oh, I am glad it is so near! But, oh, dear," he added with a sigh, "it won't be so delightful as it has been other years, because I cannot go out of doors and run and play as I have on other Christmas days."

"No but do not fret, my little son. You shall have a good time with us all here in the house," said his father.

"Oh, yes, papa, and will we have a Christmas tree? I am not too old for that. Am I?"

"No, not at all, and I doubt if you ever will be," returned his father, smoothing his shiny hair and smiling down into his face.

"Oh, Sister Gracie, will your dresses be done by that time?" asked Elsie.

"Hardly, I think," smiled Gracie, "but it will be another week before we sail away in our *Dolphin*. If they are not all finished, then they can be sent after us to Viamede."

"I suppose, grandma, you will be wanting us all at Ion for Christmas," said Ned. "Uncle Harold, do you think I will be well enough to go there for Christmas?"

"No, my boy, but we can have a fine Christmas here in your own home," replied his uncle in kindly tones.

"Oh, yes. Of course, we can. There is no place better than home, anyhow, at least, not if my grandma and you, uncle, are here with us."

"Just what I think," said Elsie. "You will be here. Won't you, grandma and uncle?"

"Part of the time," replied Mrs. Travilla, "and I think it very likely that most of your other relatives will make a call on you some time during the day."

"And you will stay with us between this time and that and tell us your nice true stories. Won't you, grandma?" entreated Ned.

"I have planned to be here a part of almost every day until we go on board the *Dolphin*,

Neddie dear," she said, smiling kindly on him as she spoke.

"And you will, too. Won't you, uncle?" queried the little fellow with an entreating look up into Harold's face.

"Yes, I intend to give my little patient all the care he needs from his doctor," was the usual pleasant-toned reply.

"Thank you, sir. That is good. I am glad I have such a kind uncle that knows how to treat sick folks," returned Ned, closing his eyes, composing himself for a nap, and adding, "I am tired and sleepy now. Please, everybody, excuse me if I do not keep awake to enjoy your company."

An hour later the little boy awoke, looking and feeling stronger and better than he had at any time since the beginning of his illness, and he continued to gain as the days passed on, listening with pleasure while his grandma and others tried to entertain him with stories and now and then joining in some quiet little game that called for no exertion of strength.

At last it was Christmas Eve, and he and Elsie went early to bed and to sleep after hanging up their stockings. They knew there was to be a Christmas tree, but the sight of it was to be deferred till the next morning. All concerned felt that after a night's rest Ned would be better able to enjoy it.

Over at Sunnyside, Evelyn sat beside the crib of her sleeping babe and was busy with her needle, fashioning a dainty robe for the darling. Lucilla stole softly in, came to her side, and speaking in an undertone so as not to disturb the little sleeper, she said, "Chester and I are going over to Woodburn to help in the trimming of the Christmas tree, and we should be very happy to have your company. Will you go along?"

"Thank you, Lu. I should like to but for leaving the baby, and I won't disturb her, by taking her up to carry her along. She is sleeping so sweetly."

"You are quite right. It would be a shame to rouse her out of that sweet sleep. The darling! How lovely she is!" responded Lucilla, leaning over the crib and feasting her eyes with a long, tender gaze into the innocent little face. "But could not you trust her to the care of her nurse for a half hour or so?"

"Thank you, but I think I am more needed here than there just now. There will be a good many to join in the fun of trimming the tree—good fun, too, it will be, I know."

"Yes, and you have already sent over your and Max's lovely gifts. Well, good-bye, sister dear. You will be missed, but no one will blame you for staying beside your darling."

Eva was missed, and her absence regretted, but the work of trimming the tree went merrily on. The captain, Violet, Harold, Gracie, Chester, and Lucilla all took part in the work, while visiting relatives came pouring in, bringing both Christmas and wedding gifts. There was a merry time, and Gracie seemed almost over-whelmed by the multitude of rare and beautiful presents—some of them very costly—bestowed upon her. There were laces, jewelry, gold and silver tableware, several handsome pictures for her walls, pretty toilet sets, books. From Harold's mother and Gracie's father there were certificates of valuable stock, which would add largely to the income of the young couple.

The tree proved to be a particularly large and handsome one when brought in, and it made a grand appearance, indeed, at the conclusion of the work of the trimmers.

There were many expressions of gleeful admiration when the work was at last completed, and then all were invited to the dining room to be treated to a feast of cakes and ices.

"Dearest, I fear this has been almost too much for you," Harold said in a low aside to his betrothed when the last of the guests had bidden adieu and departed. "I hope excitement is not going to keep you awake."

"I will try not to allow it to do so," she returned in the same low key, smiling up into his eyes. "I hope to show myself tomorrow a patient to be proud of."

"As you are tonight, love, and always," returned Harold gallantly, taking her hand and carrying it to his lips.

"In the estimation of my very partial betrothed doctor," laughed Gracie.

"Ah, yes, and in that of many others. The lover is craving a private interview with his best beloved, but the doctor knows she should at once retire to her couch for a good night's rest. Goodnight, darling. Only a week now till I can claim you for my very own."

"Goodnight, my best and dearest of physicians. I will follow your prescription, as has been my wont in the past," returned Gracie, gently withdrawing her hand from his grasp and gliding into the hall and up the stairway, while Harold moved out onto the veranda, where Captain Raymond and Violet, arm in arm, were pacing to and fro. They were chatting cozily of what they had been doing and were still to do to make the morrow a specially happy day to their children and servants. They paused in their walk at sight of Harold coming toward.

"You are not going to leave us tonight?" they asked Harold.

"Yes. I have a patient to visit, and I must hasten, for it is growing late."

"Well, come in as early as you can tomorrow," said Violet, and the captain seconded his wife's invitation warmly.

"You may be sure I will do that," laughed Harold, "both for the enjoyment of your society and the good of my patients here. Au revoir."

"Dear fellow!" exclaimed Violet, looking after him as he moved with his firm, elastic tread down the driveway and through the great gates into the road beyond. "He is worth his weight in gold, both as brother and physician, I think."

"And I am pretty much of the same opinion," smiled the captain. "Now, my dear wife, shall we go upstairs and oversee the filling of the stockings for two little dreamers?"

"Yes, for I presume the youthful owners of the stockings are already safe from disturbance in the Land of Nod. Will Gracie hang her stocking up? Do you think?"

"Hardly, I suppose, but we might steal a march upon the darling after she, too, has reached the Land of Nod."

They had passed up the stairway while they talked, and they were now near the door of Gracie's sitting room. Hearing their voices, though their tones were rather subdued for fear of waking the children, she opened it and came smilingly out.

"Ah, papa and mamma, I presume you are about the business of filling stockings, and I should like to help a little," she laughed, holding up to view a string of coral beads and a pretty purse of her own knitting.

"Ah," said her father, "those will give pleasure, I know. The children will be well satisfied with those articles. Ah, this reminds me of the first Christmas in this house, and the delight of my two daughters—Lu and Gracie—over the treasures they found in their stockings. Suppose you hang yours tonight in memory of that time."

"Oh, father dear, I have already had so many, many gifts far beyond my deserts, I should feel ashamed to be seeking more," Gracie replied with a look of ardent, filial love up into his face.

"But do you think you could be wrong or foolish in following your father's advice?" was Violet's smiling query.

"Not if it be given seriously and in earnest, mamma," returned Gracie, giving her father a look of loving inquiry.

"You may as well take it in earnest, daughter mine," he answered, drawing her to his side, putting his arm about her, and giving her a fond caress. "Should you find nothing in it of more worth than a paper of sugar plums, you will have lost nothing by the experiment. But go on now with your preparations for bed and do not let anxiety concerning the filling of the stocking keep you awake."

"Thank you, my dearest and best of fathers. I shall do my best to obey your kind order. Goodnight to you and mamma," she said, retreating into her room and closing her door. She did not fasten it, though, and laughingly hung up her stocking before getting into bed.

She was quite weary from the unusual exertion of the day and evening and in spite of excitement had presently fallen into profound slumber. Nor did she awaken till broad daylight. Then the first thing her eye fell upon was the evidently well-filled stocking. With a light laugh, she sprang out of bed, seized the stocking, crept back into bed, and began an excited examination.

There were fruits and candies and a paper parcel labeled, "A little Christmas gift from papa." Hastily opening it, she found a handsome new wallet filled with bank notes and change.

"My dear father!" she murmured to herself low and feelingly. "Was there ever such another? And mamma, too," as she picked up a pretty knitted purse, between the meshes of which shone some bright pieces of gold and silver. "But it is Christmas morning. No doubt everybody else in the house is up, and so must I be," she added half aloud, suiting the action to the word.

She was looking very sweet and fair in a pretty morning gown when, a few minutes later, her father came in, took her in his arms, and wished her, "A merry, happy Christmas, to be followed by the happiest of New Year's."

"Thank you, dear, dearest papa," she said, returning his caresses. "I feel sure it will be a happy year, because I am not to be parted from you—except for a few days till you join us on the coast of Florida."

"Yes, daughter dear, Providence permitting, we shall follow you there very shortly after you reach its shores. Now we will all go down to breakfast, which is ready and waiting for us, and after that and family worship children and servants are to see the Christmas tree and receive their gifts."

That plan was well carried out, the last act producing much mirth and jollity amid which Harold joined them. He came full of good cheer, exchanged Christmas greetings, and gave an amusing account of the Christmas doings and effect of the Christmas tree at Ion.

He and Gracie had exchanged some trifling gifts by means of the Christmas tree, but now he drew her aside and added to the ornaments she wore a beautiful diamond pin.

"Oh, thank you!" she said with a pleased little laugh. "I have a surprise for you, but this lovely brooch quite casts it into the shade."

As she spoke, she drew from her pocket a tiny box and put it into his hand. He opened it and found a diamond stud.

"Ah, what a beauty!" he exclaimed in tones of pleased surprise. "Thank you, my darling. Thank you a thousand times. It is valuable in itself and still more valuable as the gift of my best beloved of earthly dear ones."

"I am very glad you like my little gift," she returned, smiling up into his eyes. "Though it compares but poorly with this lovely and costly one you have given me. Oh, but it is a beauty! I must show it to papa, mamma, and the rest."

"Show us what?" asked Violet, overhearing the last few words and turning toward the speaker.

"This, that your good, generous brother has just added to my already rich store of Christmas gifts," replied Gracie, joyously displaying her new treasure.

"Oh, what a beauty!" cried Violet. "I am glad, Harold, that you show such good taste and generosity to the dear girl you are stealing from us."

"I object to that clause of your speech," returned her brother with mock gravity. "It will be no theft, since her father has made it a gift in generous gratitude for my small services to your small son."

"Oh, true enough," laughed Violet, "and our saved son is worth more than any quantity of such jewelry," she added in moved tones, putting an arm around Ned, who had stolen to her side in an effort to see what had caused her pleased exclamation.

"Oh, what a beautiful pin, Gracie!" he exclaimed. "Did you buy it for her, uncle?"

"Yes, on purpose for her," replied Harold, smiling down at the little fellow. "You do not think it too fine for her. Do you?"

"No, no. Oh, no! Nothing could be too fine for our dear, sweet, beautiful Gracie."

"Just what papa thinks," the captain said, joining the little group. "Ah," glancing through the window, "here come our Sunnyside folks to spend the day with us."

Visits from other relatives followed somewhat later, and some who had not been heard from the day before brought additions to the store of wedding and Christmas gifts. Ned was not forgotten or neglected, and in spite of having to remain at home and within doors, he passed a very happy Christmas Day.

CHAPTER FOURTH

THAT CHRISTMAS WEEK was a very busy and cheery one to the Woodburn folk and their near and dear ones on the neighboring estates. The Fairview family were expecting to spend the rest of the winter at Viamede. Cousin Ronald and his Annis had accepted a cordial invitation to do likewise, and Grandma Elsie's brother and his family from the Oaks would also pay her a visit there, the duration of which was not settled, as that would depend upon how well Horace's affairs at home should be carried on without his presence and supervision. His little daughter Elsie was to make one of the party on the yacht, but the others would go by rail, as that would not necessitate so early a start from home. The *Dolphin* was being put into readiness for her trip, and the overseeing of that business occupied quite a portion of Captain Raymond's time during that week.

Gracie made a lovely bride surrounded by all her own and Harold's kith and kin. The ceremony took place at noon. A grand dinner followed, and then wedding attire was exchanged for a pretty and becoming traveling suit.

Carriages conveyed bride, groom, his mother, and their young charges to the *Dolphin*, and presently the southward journey was fairly begun.

It had been rather hard for Ned to part from his papa and mamma for even a few days. Though with dear grandma and uncle left to him, sister and cousins also, and wearied with that grief and the exciting scenes of the day, he was soon ready to take to his berth and fall asleep.

The others found it too cool for comfort on the deck, but it was very pleasant in the well warmed and lighted salon. They sat and chatted there for some little time, but soon all retired to their staterooms for the night.

The morning found Ned refreshed and strengthened and the rest in fine health and spirits. They made a cheerful, merry little company about the breakfast table, and afterward they took some exercise on the deck and then gathered about Grandma Elsie in the salon and pleaded for one of her "lovely stories."

"Well, dears, what shall I tell of?" she asked with her own sweet smile. "Something more of our Washington or of others of our presidents?"

"Oh, tell us about the time of our Civil War and the pictures Nast drew then," cried Elsie excitedly. "I saw something about him and his drawings the other day, and I should like to know more of him and his wonderful work. Was he an American, grandma?"

"No, my dear. He was born in the military barracks of Landau, a little fortified town of Germany, and came to this country at the age of six. He and his sister were brought here by their mother. The husband and father was then on a French man-of-war. Afterward he enlisted on an American vessel, but he could not join his family until Thomas, his son, was ten years old, and mother and children had been four years in this country. A comrade of his told them he was coming, and the news made a great excitement in the family.

"The mother sent Thomas to buy a cake with which to welcome his father. As he was coming home with that, he was passed by a closed cab. It suddenly stopped, and a man sprang out, caught him up, and put him in the cab then got in himself. For an instant, Thomas was frightened, thinking he was kidnapped. Then he found he was in his father's arms and was full of joy. But he was troubled when he saw that between them they had crushed the cake. He thought his mother would be greatly disappointed by that. But she was so glad to see her husband that she did not seem to mind it—the damage to the cake. Nor did the children, being so delighted to see their father and the many presents he had brought them all from distant places and to listen to all he had to tell about his travels.

"Thomas was a short, stout, moon-faced lad. He attended a German school for a short time after his father came home, but he was constantly drawing pictures. His teacher would say to him, 'Go finish your picture, Nast. You will never learn to read.' Often, he would draw a file of soldiers or a pair of prize fighters—sometimes things he remembered from his life in Landau, such as a little girl with her pet lamb or old Santa Claus with his pack.

"In 1860, he went to England, where he still made drawings. Every steamer brought letters from him and papers to the *New York News*. From England he went, that very same year, to Italy to join Garibaldi."

"Who was Garibaldi, grandma, and what did Nast want to join him for?" asked Ned.

"To help him get Italy free," replied Mrs. Travilla. "But I will not tell the story of Garibaldi now—some other time, perhaps. The war was not very long, and Nast stayed until it was over. In November of that same year, he said good-bye to his friends in Italy. Then he visited Rome, Florence, and Genoa. Late in December, he reached Landau—his native city. The old place had not changed, except that to him it looked much smaller than it had before. He went on through Germany, visiting art galleries and cathedrals. But he grew tired of it all and wanted to get home. He crossed the channel to England, and there he heard talk of the brewing of war in this country, now his own land. He stayed a few days in London but then sailed for the United States, which he reached on February first of 1861. He had been gone a year, and he now arrived in New York with only a dollar and a half in his pocket."

"Oh, how little after such long, hard work!" exclaimed Elsie Raymond.

"Yes," said Mrs. Travilla, "but he was brave and industrious and went on working as before. Mr. Lincoln had been elected to the presidency the November before, and in March, Nast went to Washington to see his inauguration."

A portfolio lay on the table beside which Mrs. Travilla now sat, and she took it up and opened it, saying, "I have some articles in this which I have been saving for years past, among them some things about Nast—some of his own writing. I have taken an interest in him ever since the time of our Civil War. Listen to this, which was written at the time when Lincoln was about to be inaugurated. Nast had been ordered by his newspaper—the *New York News*—to go to Washington to see the inaugural ceremony. Stopping in Philadelphia, he was near Lincoln during the celebrated speech and flag-raising at Independence Hall, and afterward he heard the address Lincoln made from the balcony of the Continental Hotel.

"At Washington, Nast stopped at the Willard Hotel, which was Lincoln's headquarters. A feeling of shuddering horror, such as a bad dream sometimes gives us, came over him there. The men who had sworn that 'Abe Lincoln' should not take his seat were not gone. Now I will read you what he says about that time."

All of the children sat very still, listening quite attentively to the narrative—Elsie Raymond with an almost breathless interest in it—while her grandmother read.

"'It seemed to me that the shadow of death was everywhere. I had endless visions of black funeral parades accompanied by mournful music. It was as if the whole city were mined, and I know now that it was figuratively true. A single yell of defiance would have inflamed a mob. A shot would have started a conflict. In my room at the Willard Hotel, I was trying to work. I picked up my pencils and laid them down as many as a dozen times. I got up at last and walked the floor. Presently in the rooms next to mine, other men were walking, too. I could hear them in the silence. My head was beginning to throb, and I sat down and pressed my hands to my temples. Then all at once, in the Ebbett House, across the way, a window was flung up and a man stepped out on the balcony. The footsteps about me ceased. Everybody had heard the man and was waiting breathlessly to see what he would do. Suddenly, in a rich, powerful voice he began to sing *The Star-Spangled Banner*. The result was extraordinary. Windows were thrown up. Crowds gathered on the streets. A multitude of voices joined the song. When it was over the street rang with cheers. The men in the rooms next to mine joined me in the corridor. The hotel came to life. Guests wept and flung their arms about one another. Dissension and threats were silenced. It seemed to me, and I believe to all of us, that Washington had been saved by the inspiration of an unknown man with a voice to sing that grand old song of songs.'"

"Who was that man, grandma?" asked Ned.

"I can't tell you that, Neddie," she replied. "I think it has never been known who he was."

"Are there some more stories about Nast and his pictures?" he asked

"Yes. He made a great many more pictures. One, on the first page of the Christmas *Harper*, was called 'Santa Claus.' It showed him dressed in the stars and stripes, distributing presents in the military camps. In the same paper was another called 'Christmas Eve.' It had two parts—one, in a large wreath, was a picture of the soldier's family at home; and in another wreath was the soldier by the campfire, looking at a picture of his wife and children. Letters came from all parts of the Union with thanks for that picture. A colonel wrote that it reached him on Christmas Eve and that he had unfolded it by the light of his campfire and wept over it. 'It was only a picture,' he said, 'but I couldn't help it.'"

"I don't wonder," sighed Elsie softly, "for how he must have wanted to be at home with his wife and children."

Harold and Gracie, who had been taking their morning exercise upon the deck, returned to the salon and joined the group of listeners just in time to hear their mother's story of Nast's Christmas pictures.

"Nast certainly did a great deal for the Union cause," said Harold. "Do you remember, mother, what Grant said of him when asked, 'Who is the greatest single figure in civil life developed by the Civil War?'"

"Yes. He answered without a moment's hesitation, 'Thomas Nast. He did as much as any one man to bring the war to an end.' And many of the Northern generals and statesmen held that same opinion."

"Yes, mother. All lovers of the Union certainly owe him a debt of gratitude."

"Now, children, shall I tell you something about Lincoln?" she asked. There was an eager assent, and she went on. "He was a noble, unselfish, Christian man. He came to the Presidency in a dark and stormy time and did all in his power to avert civil war without allowing the destruction of the Union, denying the right of any state or number of states to go out of the Union. But the rebellious states would not listen, declared themselves out of the Union, began seizing government property, and firing upon those who had it in charge. Lincoln was finally compelled to call out troops for its defense.

"But I shall not go over the whole sad story now. After four years, when it was all over, every loyal heart was full of joy, and Lincoln's praise was on every tongue. They felt that he had saved his country and theirs at the expense of great suffering to himself. Only a few days later, he was fatally shot by a bad fellow, an actor named John Wilkes Booth."

"Was he one of the Confederates, grandma?" asked Ned.

"I think not," she replied. "It is said that his controlling motive for the dreadful deed was insane conceit. For weeks beforehand, he had declared his purpose to do something that would make his name ring around the world."

"As it has," remarked Harold, "but in such a way as I should think no sane man would desire for his name to be repeated."

"And did they hang him?" asked Ned.

"No," replied his uncle, "the awful crime was so sudden and unexpected that for several minutes the audience did not comprehend what had been done, and the assassin escaped for a time. He ran out, leaped upon a saddled horse kept waiting for him, and galloped away into the country. He rode into Maryland, from there into Virginia, and took refuge in a barn. He was pursued. Cavalry surrounded the barn, and they called upon him and his companion to surrender. The other man did, but Booth refused and offered to fight the captain and his men. They set the barn on fire, and one of them, against orders, shot Booth in the neck. That shot made him helpless. He was carried out, laid on the grass, and after four hours of intense agony, he died."

"That was a very sad, sad time," sighed Mrs. Travilla. "The whole North was in mourning for Lincoln, and even the South soon saw that it had lost a good friend. There was a movement of sympathy for our nation in its great loss throughout the world."

"Yes, mother," said Harold, "and time seem only to increase the esteem of the world for that great and good man."

CHAPTER FIFTH

THE NEXT DAY, after some healthful exercise upon the deck, the children returned to the salon. Gathering about Grandma Elsie, they begged for another story.

"Something historical?" she asked with her pleasant smile.

"Yes, grandma, if you please," replied Elsie Ryamond. "I liked your story of Marion so much and should be glad to hear about some other Revolutionary soldier who helped to drive away the British."

"Well, if you would all like that, I will tell you of Sergeant Jasper and his brave doings."

The other children gave an eager assent, and Mrs. Travilla began.

"History tells us that William Jasper was born in South Carolina in 1750. That would make him about twenty-six years old when the Revolutionary War began. He was patriotic, and at once he enlisted as a sergeant in the Second South Carolina Regiment.

"In June of 1776, a British fleet appeared off Charleston bar, and several hundred land troops took possession of Long Island, which was separated from Sullivan—on which was our Fort Sullivan—only by a narrow creek. At half past ten o'clock on the morning of the twenty-eighth of June, the British ships anchored in front of our Fort Sullivan, which instantly poured a heavy fire upon them.

"But I shall not go into a detailed account of the battle, which, Lossing tells us, was one of the severest during the whole war, redounded to the military glory of the Americans, greatly increased the patriotic strength at the South, and was regarded by the British as very disastrous. The loss of life on their ship was frightful.

"But I must tell you of a daring feat performed by Sergeant Jasper. At the beginning of the action, the flag staff of our fort was cut away by a ball from a British ship, and the crescent flag of South Carolina that waved opposite the Union flag upon the western bastion fell outside upon the beach. Jasper leaped the parapet, walked the length of the fort, picked up the flag, fastened it upon a sponge staff, and in the sight of the whole British fleet, whose iron hail was pouring upon the fortress, he fixed the flag firmly upon the bastion. Then he climbed up to the parapet and leaped, unhurt, within the fort, three cheers greeting him as he did so."

"Oh, how brave he was!" cried Ned. "I hope they gave him a reward for it."

"Yes," said his grandma, "the governor, on the day after the battle, visited the fort, and he rewarded Jasper with the gift of his own small sword, a handsome one which hung by his side. The governor thanked him in the name of his country. He also offered him a lieutenant's commission, but the young hero declined it, saying, 'I am not fit to keep officers' company. I am but a sergeant, sir.'

"It would seem that he had had no educational advantages, as he could neither read nor write."

"What a pity!" exclaimed several young voices.

"Yes, it was," sighed Mrs. Travilla. "I hope you are thankful, my dears, for the superior advantages that each of you enjoy.

"I have read that Jasper was given a roving commission, and choosing six men from the regiment to go with him, he went here and there and often returned with prisoners before his general even knew of his absence.

"Jasper had a brother who had joined the British, but he loved him so dearly that he ventured into the British garrison to see him. The brother was greatly alarmed at sight of him, lest he should be seized and hung as an American spy, his name being well known to many of the British officers. But Jasper said, 'Don't trouble yourself. I am no longer an American soldier.'

"'Thank God for that, William!' exclaimed the brother, giving him a hearty shake of the hand. 'Now only say the word, my boy, and here is a commission for you with regimentals and gold to boot to fight for his Majesty, King George.'

"But Jasper shook his head, saying that though there seemed but little encouragement to fight for his country, he could not fight against her. He stayed two or three days with his brother, hearing and seeing all that he could. He then bade good-bye and returned to the American camp by a circuitous route and told General Lincoln all that he had seen."

"Grandma," said Ned thoughtfully, "it seems to me he did not tell the truth when he said he was not an American soldier. Was it right for him to say that?"

"I think not, Ned. But I suppose he thought it was, as he meant by it to help his country's cause. But remember, my dears, it is never right to do evil even that good may come.

"But to go on with my story. Jasper soon went again to the English garrison, this time taking with him his particular friend, Sergeant Newton, who was a young man of great strength and courage. Jasper's brother received them very cordially, and they remained several days at the British fort without causing the least alarm.

"On the morning of the third day, the brother said to them, 'I have bad news to tell you.' 'Aye, what is it?' asked William. His brother replied that a dozen prisoners had been brought in that morning as deserters from Savannah. They were to be sent there immediately, and from all he could learn, it would be likely to go hard with them, as it seemed they had taken the King's bounty."

"What does that mean, grandma?" asked Ned.

"That they had agreed to remain loyal British subjects instead of fighting for their country. For that, the British were to protect them against the Americans. But it seems they had changed their minds and gone over to the cause of their country.

"Jasper asked to see the poor fellows, and his brother took him and Newton to the spot where the poor fellows were, handcuffed, sitting or lying upon the ground. With them was a young woman, a wife of one of the prisoners, sitting on the ground opposite to her husband with her little boy leaning on her lap. Her dress showed that she was poor, and her coal-black hair spread in long, neglected tresses on her neck and bosom. Sometimes she would sit silent, like a statue of grief, her eyes fixed upon the ground. Then she would start convulsively, lift her eyes, and gaze on her husband's face with a terribly sad look as if she already saw him struggling in the halter, herself a widow, and her child an orphan. The child was evidently distressed by his mother's anguish, and he was weeping with her.

"Jasper and Newton felt keenly for them in their misery. They silently walked away into a neighboring wood with tears in both of their eyes. Jasper presently spoke. 'Newton,' he said, 'my days have been but few, but I believe their course is nearly finished.' Newton asked why he thought so, and he answered because he felt that he must rescue those prisoners or die with them, otherwise the remembrance of that poor woman and her child would haunt him to his grave.

"'That is exactly what I feel, too,' replied Newton. 'Here is my hand and heart to stand by you, my brave friend, to the last drop. Thank God, a man can die but once, and why should we fear to leave this life in the way of our duty?'

"Then the two embraced each other and at once set about making the necessary arrangements for carrying out their desperate resolution."

"Oh, how brave and kind those two men were!" exclaimed Elsie Raymond. "I am proud of them as my countrymen."

"As we all may be," said her grandma. Then she went on with her story.

"Shortly after breakfast the next morning, the prisoners were sent on their way to Savannah. They were guarded by a sergeant and a corporal with eight men."

"Why, that was ten men for our two men to fight!" exclaimed Elsie Dinsmore.

"But I hope our brave fellows didn't give it up," said Elsie Raymond.

"No," replied her grandma. "Jasper presently took leave of his brother, and he and Newton started on some pretended errand to the upper country. As soon as they were fairly out of sight of the town, they struck into the woods and hurried after the prisoners and guards, keeping out of sight in the bushes and anxiously watching for an opportunity to strike a blow.

"I think that to most men it would have seemed great folly for two unarmed men to attempt to strike a blow at ten men carrying loaded muskets and bayonets. But they were very brave and not at all willing to give up their countrymen to the dreadful fate the cruel British had appointed for them.

"Jasper said to Newton, 'Perhaps the guard may stop at the Spa to quench their thirst, and we may be able to attack them there.'

"The Spa! What was that, grandma?" asked Ned excitedly.

"The Spa is a famous spring that is about two miles from Savannah, where travelers often stopped for a drink of its good water, Ned," she replied pleasantly.

"Jasper and Newton hurried on and concealed themselves among the bushes that grew thickly around the spring.

"Soon the soldiers and the prisoners came into sight of it, and the sergeant ordered a halt. That gave our heroes a little hope, though the odds were fearful against them. The corporal, with his guard of four men, led the prisoners to the spring, while the sergeant, with the other four, grounded their arms near the road then brought up the rear. The prisoners, wearied with their long walk, were permitted to rest themselves on the earth. Mrs. Jones took her seat opposite her husband as usual, and her tired little boy fell asleep on her lap. Two of the corporal's men were ordered to keep guard and the other two to give the prisoners a drink out of their canteens. They obeyed, drew near the spring, rested their muskets against a pine tree, then dipped up the water, drank, filled their canteens again and turned to give the prisoners a drink.

"'Now, Newton, is our time,' whispered Jasper. With that, they sprang from their concealment, snatched up the two muskets resting against the tree, and in an instant shot down the two soldiers who were upon guard. The other two Englishmen sprang forward and seized their muskets. But before they could use them, Jasper and Newton with clubbed guns leveled a blow at their heads and broke their skulls. Down they sank, pale and quivering, without even a groan. Then snatching up the muskets, our heroes flew between the other British soldiers and their arms, grounded near the road, and ordered them to surrender, which they immediately did. Then they—our men—snapped the handcuffs off the prisoners and armed them with muskets."

"Oh, how good!" exclaimed Ned and all the little girls who were listening to Grandma Elsie's story of the Revolution.

"But what did Mrs. Jones do while that fight was going on?" asked Elsie Dinsmore.

"At the beginning of it, she fainted," replied Mrs. Travilla, "and her little son stood screaming piteously over her. But when she recovered her senses and saw her husband and his friends freed from their fetters, she seemed frantic with joy. She sprang to her husband, and, with her arms about his neck, sobbed out, 'My husband is safe, bless God! My husband is safe!' Then snatching up her child, she pressed him to her heart, exclaiming, 'Thank God, my son has a father yet.' Then kneeling at the feet of Jasper and

Newton, she pressed their hands vehemently, but so full was her heart that all she could say was, 'God bless you. God Almighty bless you.'"

"Oh, how nice!" exclaimed Ned, clapping his hands in delight.

"Then what did they all do, grandma?" asked Elsie Raymond. "Not go to Savannah, I suppose, as the British were there?"

"No. They recrossed the Savannah River, taking the arms and regimentals of the dead, their prisoners, too, and safely joined the American army at Parisburg, where they were received with great astonishment and joy."

"No wonder there was astonishment," said Elsie Raymond, "that two men could beat ten."

"That was because the two were Americans and the others were only Englishmen," chuckled Ned. "Is there any more to that story about Jasper, grandma?"

"Not much," she replied. "He was killed at the siege of Savannah in 1779. Several gallant defenders of the French and American colors had been shot down. Sergeant Jasper sprang forward, seized the standards, and kept them erect. Then he, too, was prostrated by a bullet and fell into the ditch. He was carried to the camp and soon died. Jasper's name is honored in Savannah. They have made that evident by bestowing it upon one of the city's squares."

CHAPTER SIXTH

IT WAS SABBATH MORNING, and the little party on the yacht was gathered about the breakfast table, Dr. Harold having just come down from the deck, where he had spent the last few minutes.

"What of the weather, Harold?" asked his mother quietly.

"It is cool and cloudy," he said in reply, "rather too cool and damp for ladies and children to pass much time on deck, I think, mother. I may gather the men there and read them a sermon, but the rest of you, I hope, will be content to pass at least most of the day in these lower, warmer quarters."

"I think we can pass the day very contentedly, if mother will lead us in some Bible lessons," said Gracie with a loving, smiling look at her whom, until of late, she had been wont to call Grandma Elsie.

"Very willingly, daughter mine," was the sweet-toned, smiling assent, which was received by all the children with looks and words of pleased anticipation.

On leaving the table, they had family worship in the salon, Dr. Harold leading the service. Then he went upon the deck, and the others gathered about Grandma Elsie.

Elsie Raymond, sitting there with her Bible in hand, exclaimed eagerly, "Oh, grandma, I am glad of this opportunity to ask you about what I have been reading here, this miracle of the Lord Jesus feeding so many, many folks—five thousand men, besides women and children—on only five loaves and two fishes. It couldn't have been nearly enough, except by Jesus blessing it and making it more. Could it, grandma?"

"No, indeed, Elsie. Five large loaves, such as you are accustomed to seeing, would hardly be enough to feed fifty such hungry men. These five loaves were much smaller than ours—probably little, if any, larger than our soda crackers. They would hardly have been enough to satisfy the appetite of one hungry boy."

"There were two fishes besides, you know, grandma. But if they were small ones, a boy could eat them, too."

"Yes. So it should be no wonder that the disciples thought it utterly impossible to feed that great crowd of hungry people and begged Jesus to send them away to go into the villages and buy themselves food to eat."

"Do you suppose they had any money to buy it with, grandma?" asked the little girl.

"I think it probable that most of them were poor people with little or no money about them," replied Grandma Elsie. "And even if they had money, there were too many to find sufficient food in the little nearby towns. Jesus knew all that. He could see how weary and hungry many, if not all of them, were, particularly the women and little children. Jesus pitied them and was ready to help them as no one else could, and no doubt He was glad He had the power. He bade His disciples not to tell them to depart, but 'Give ye them to eat,' He said. They replied, 'We have here but five loaves and two fishes;' and Jesus said, 'Bring them hither to me.' John tells us there was much grass in the place, and that the men sat down in numbers of about five thousand. Then He (Jesus) took the five loaves and the two fishes, and looking up to heaven, He blessed and broke the loaves and gave them to the disciples, and they distributed them among the great multitude. All ate until they were satisfied. Then Jesus said, 'Gather up the fragments that remain, that nothing be lost.' John tells us, 'Therefore, they gathered them together and filled twelve baskets with the fragments of the five barley loaves, which remained over and above unto them that had eaten.'"

"It was a very wonderful miracle, grandma. Wasn't it?" asked the little girl thoughtfully.

"Yes, indeed! A miracle that none but God could work. It proved that Jesus was divine. You have been reading Matthew's account of this miracle. Now turn to the sixth chapter of Mark, and you will find the same story told by him. Then in the eighth chapter, we will find that he tells of another time when Jesus had worked a similar miracle—when He fed four thousand on seven loaves and a few small fishes. They also took up the broken meat and bread and that which was left filled seven baskets."

"Yes, grandma," said the little girl, turning over the leaves of her Bible, "and it says after that first time that He departed into a mountain to pray. But after the second, 'and straightway He entered into a ship with His disciples, and came into the parts of Dalmanutha.' Where was that place, grandma?"

"It was a town on the west coast of the sea of Galilee. Read on now to the eleventh verse."

Elsie read, "'And the Pharisees came forth and began to question Him, seeking of Him a sign from heaven, tempting Him. And He sighed deeply in His spirit, and said, "Why doth this generation seek after a sign? Verily I say unto you, There shall no sign be given unto this generation." And He left them, and entering into the ship, again departed to the other side.'"

"Weren't the bad men wanting to do Jesus harm?" asked Ned.

"Yes, they were, indeed," replied his grandma. "They hated Him because He told them of their sins. '"Woe unto you, scribes and Pharisees, hypocrites! For ye are as graves which appear not, and the men that walk over them are not aware of them."' Then to the people: '"Beware ye of the leaven of the Pharisees, which is hypocrisy."' Again He said of them: '"In vain do they worship Me, teaching for doctrines the commandments of men . . . Woe unto you, lawyers! for ye have taken away the key of knowledge: ye entered not in yourselves, and them that were entering in ye hindered."' And as He said these unto them, the scribes and Pharisees began to urge Him vehemently, and to provoke Him to speak of many things; laying wait for Him, and seeking to catch something out of His mouth, that they might accuse Him. They were angry and wanted to kill Jesus, because He exposed their wickedness. In another chapter we are told, 'And He went into the temple and began to cast out them that sold therein, and them that bought; Saying unto them, "It is written, My house is the house of prayer: but ye have made it a den of thieves." And He taught daily in the temple. But the chief priests and the scribes and the chief of the people sought to destroy Him, and could not find what they might do: for all the people were very attentive to hear Him.'"

"So they went out at night, when the crowds of people who loved Him were in their homes and asleep, I suppose, the wicked, money-loving Judas showing them where He was, and led Him away to the high priest and all the chief priests and the elders and the scribes," sighed Elsie Raymond sadly.

"Yes," said her grandma, "and they went through a mock trial, but they could not get their witnesses to agree. And the high priest stood up in the midst and asked Jesus, saying, '"Answerest thou nothing? What is it which these witness against thee?" But Jesus made no answer. Again the high priest asked him, "Art thou the Christ, the Son of the Blessed?" Jesus said, "I am; and ye shall see the Son of man sitting on the right hand of power, and coming in the clouds of heaven." Then the high priest rent his clothes and saith, "What need we any further witnesses? Ye have heard the blasphemy: what think ye?" And they all condemned Him to be guilty of death. And some began to spit on Him, and to cover His face, and to buffet Him, and to say unto Him, "Prophesy:" and the servants did strike Him with the palms of their hands.'"

"He could have struck them all dead without a word. Couldn't He, grandma?" asked Ned.

"Indeed He could have," she replied, "but in His great love for you and for me and all His people, He chose to bear it all—all that and all the awful agony of the death upon the cross that we might be saved. The Bible tells us, 'Believe on the Lord Jesus Christ and thou shalt be saved.' The dear Savior, who died that awful death for us, invites us all to come to Him and be saved. 'For God so loved the world, that He gave His only begotten Son, that whosoever believeth in Him should not perish, but have everlasting life.' Those are His own words, spoken to Nicodemus as He explained how to be saved."

"Grandma, couldn't Jesus have hindered those wicked men from treating Him so? Couldn't He have made them all die that minute if He had chosen to?" asked Ned.

"Yes, he could, but as I have just told you, He bore it all and the awful death on the cross, so that we might be saved—we and all who would give themselves to Him. The Bible says Christ died for our sins according to the Scriptures. He took upon Himself our human nature that He might bear our punishment and save us from eternal death."

"All His earthly life long He had been looking forward to that awful, agonizing death," sighed Gracie in tones tremulous with emotion. "Oh, how could anyone help loving Him with all their hearts?"

"And strive to be like Him," added Grandma Elsie. "He was so unselfish, so forbearing and forgiving. Think of His loving, cheering, sympathizing talk with His disciples that very night in which He was betrayed and His awful suffering began. Remember, He knew all the agony He was to go through that very night—in the garden of Gethsemane, where He prayed in so great an agony that His sweat became as it were great drops of blood falling down upon the ground. After that came the betrayal, arrest, trial before the Jewish authorities with all the abuse heaped upon Him there. Then in the morning came the trial before Pilate and Herod, the scourging, the clothing with the purple robe and crown of thorns, the mocking salutation, 'Hail, King of the Jews,' the smiting of His head with the reed they had put in His right hand, the mocking bowing of the knees, and the spitting upon Him. Then He was led out wearing the purple robe and crown of thorns to the shrill cry of the chief priests and officers, 'Crucify Him! Crucify Him! Away with Him! Away with Him! Crucify Him!'"

Grandma Elsie paused, and her eyes filled with tears, her lips trembling with emotion.

"Oh, how wonderful it was that Jesus bore it all when even without a word He could have made every one of those dreadful persecutors die," said Elsie Dinsmore.

"Yes," said her aunt. "His love and compassion for us sinners was wonderfully great. Oh, how we should love Him and how carefully we should obey all His commandments! Ah, how sweet it is to belong to Him! 'Since He is mine and I am His, what can I want beside.'"

"Grandma, I want to belong to Him," said Alie Leland. "How shall I get to be His and know that I am?"

"Give yourself to Him, dear child, asking Him to make you just what He would have you to be. His promise is, 'Him that cometh to Me I will in no wise cast out.' And who shall doubt His own word? How kind and forgiving He was! Peter, who had denied Him and then repented with bitter weeping, seems to have been one of the first to whom He appeared after His resurrection. You remember, the angel whom the woman found sitting in the tomb said to them, '"Go tell His disciples and Peter."'"

"And if we are really His disciples, we will be forgiven, too. Won't we, grandma?" said Elsie Raymond quietly.

"Yes. We will ask Him to help us to be so, and He will."

"Grandma," said Ned, "wasn't it strange that when Jesus could make food so easily He should say to His disciples, '"Gather up the fragments that remain, that nothing be lost"'?"

"I think it was to teach us all that waste is sinful and that nothing which could be made useful to us or to anyone else should be thrown away. Let us take the lesson to heart and carefully obey it and every teaching of our dear Lord and master," was the gentle, sweet-toned reply, the eyes of the speaker shining with love to Him of whom she spoke and joy that she was His very own for time and for eternity.

CHAPTER SEVENTH

"WHERE ARE WE now, uncle? Have we come down to Florida, yet?" asked Ned at the breakfast table.

"Yes. We are now moving along down the east coast of that state," replied Harold. "Now we may as well decide at which and how many of its ports we will call. Should you enjoy visiting St. Augustine and Fort Marion again, Elsie?" he queried with a look of amusement at his niece.

"Oh, no, indeed, uncle!" was the quick, emphatic reply, which was accompanied by a little shiver, as if the very name brought some unpleasant recollection.

"But why not?" asked Elsie Dinsmore with a look of surprise and curiosity.

"Oh," exclaimed Elsie Raymond, "it's a very dreadful place over three hundred years old with dungeons where people used to be tortured long, long ago, and we seemed to hear one of them saying, 'Here have I lain for three hundred years with none to pity or help. Oh, 'tis a weary while! Shall I never escape?'"

"But as Cousin Ronald is not with us now we needn't fear a repetition of that," remarked Dr.

Harold reassuringly. "Still, perhaps we may as well pass St. Augustine by this time and visit places or things we did not look at before. Mother, what do you say to seeing something of the sponging business?"

"That would be instructive and probably quite interesting," was the pleased reply.

"Sponging business!" echoed Ned. "What does that mean?"

"The work of gathering sponges and making them ready for the market," replied his uncle.

"Oh, I think that would be interesting!" cried the little fellow. "Do they grow down under the water, and are they nice and clean when they are brought up, uncle?"

"Not very, Ned," replied Dr. Harold, smiling kindly upon his young questioner, "but with your grandma's help I think I can give you all needed information on the subject. Afterward, you may be able to see for yourself."

"Oh, that'll be good! Will you tell me about it, grandma?" asked Ned, turning excitedly to her.

"Sonny boy, we will have a nice talk about it in the salon after our family worship," Mrs. Travilla replied in her usual kindly tone.

"And I am sure we will all be glad to hear whatever you can tell us on the subject, mother," said Gracie. "I know it will be interesting to me and a good preparation for the sight of the spongers' work."

The two Elsies and Alie Leland expressed their pleasure in the prospect of both the information promised by Grandma Elsie and the afterward sight of the doings of the spongers.

"I think, if it suits you, mother," said Dr. Harold, "we will have our talk on the sponging subject before our morning exercises upon the deck. Sitting still for a while will aid the digestion of this hearty breakfast, and the sun will make the deck a little warmer for us afterward."

Everybody seemed pleased with that plan, and it was carried out, Dr. Harold making one of his mother's little audience.

"Have you a map of Florida, Harold?" she asked.

"Oh, yes, mother, I have," he replied, "also some pictures that will be helpful." He hastened to his stateroom and brought them out.

"Ah, these will be quite a help," she said. "Come, children, let us look at the map first." Then as they gathered around the table on which she had laid the map, she said, "There, on the east coast, near the southern end of the state, you see Miami, and starting from a point near it a chain of keys, or islands, begins which extends in the shape of a horn down into the Gulf of Mexico, the Dry Tortugas being the westernmost. Sponges are found in the waters surrounding most of these keys, also between them and the mainland as far as Cape Sable. This is called 'the key grounds.' Some of the people living on the larger islands and spongers from Key West are the only persons who engage in that work there. In the Gulf of Mexico, on the west coast, are the 'bay grounds,' which yield the most. They extend from John's Pass, a few miles north of the entrance to Tampa Bay, all the way down to St. Mark's Lighthouse."

"How far is that, grandma?" asked Ned.

"How far, Harold?" she asked.

"About two hundred miles, I think, mother," he replied.

"There are some sponges to be found between Tampa Bay and Cape Sable, but not enough to make it worthwhile to take special trips to that point," she continued.

"Now, who here can tell me whether it is to the vegetable or animal kingdom that the sponge belongs?"

"Oh, grandma," laughed Ned, "I'm sure a sponge isn't an animal."

"Are you?" she queried with an amused smile. "Now, little girls, what are your opinions in regard to the matter?"

"Why, I never thought of a sponge as being either an animal or a vegetable!" exclaimed Alie Leland. "Which is it, grandma?"

"It actually belongs to the animal kingdom," was the reply. "I have never seen it in its natural state, but from what I have read and heard I know it is a very different-looking object from what it becomes in being prepared for the market. When first brought up from the water, it looks something like a jellyfish or mass of liver, as its entire surface is covered with a thin, slimy skin, usually of a dark color, having openings into what we call the holes of the sponge. What we call a sponge is really only the skeleton of one."

"And men go down into deep water to get them. Do they?" queried Ned.

"Do you know how deep the water is on this coast, Harold?" asked his mother.

"I have been told from ten to fifty feet here in Florida, mother, but it is considerably more in the Mediterranean Sea. The finest grades of sponge are found in the deepest water. Sponges from the sea are said to be superior in quality to those found in either Florida or the West Indies."

"Go on, son, and give us all the information you can," said his mother as he paused.

"If you wish, mother," he replied with an affectionate look and smile. "In the waters of Florida and the West Indies the fishing is done in flat-bottomed boats called dinghies. A tin or wooden pail with a glass bottom is used to help locate the sponges by lowering it into the water and looking down through it. When that has been done, they are brought up by means of a pole some thirty feet long with a sharp, curved, double hook, with which they, the sponges, are detached and drawn up to the surface. When the spongers have gotten a boatload, they lay the sponges out to decompose in a kraal on the beach, where it is washed by the sea. At that time, the odor is very unpleasant. When they have been in the kraal about a week, they are beaten out with a short, heavy stick, which removes most of the slime and animal matter still remaining in them. Where the black scum still adheres, they are scraped with a knife. The sponges are next squeezed out right thoroughly with the hands and taken to the shore and strung on pieces of coarse twine about six feet long, and then they are ready for sale by auction."

"What is a kraal, uncle?" asked Ned.

"It is a pen, generally about ten feet square, built of wattled stakes, and it is placed in shallow water near some key or island," relied Dr. Harold. "Here is a picture of one," he added, taking it from the table and holding it out so that all could see.

It was gazed upon with interest. Then several other pictures were shown, examined, and commented upon interestedly—one or two spongers at work on the water, one of them with the long, hooked pole, the other gazing through the bucket with the glass bottom.

Another picture was of the sponge yard at Key West, showing the sponges drying. There were pictures of sponge auctions, too, and of a boat bringing sponges to the wharf at Key West.

"And can we see all these things when we get there—to Key West, I mean?" asked Ned. Then he added, "I think it would be a good deal better—more interesting—to look at them than only at their pictures."

"I hope to give you that pleasure, Neddie boy," replied his uncle, smiling on him and patting his cheek. "We will very likely have to wait a day or two at Key West for your father and mother and the rest who are to join us there and pass with us through the Gulf of Mexico on the way to Viamede."

"Is there a town there, uncle?" asked Elsie.

"Yes, a well-built town with quite wide streets crossing at right angles, and having churches, schools, and a fine Marine Hospital belonging to the United States."

"Hotels, too, I suppose," remarked Elsie Dinsmore, "but we won't care for them, having this delightful yacht to stay in."

"No, and in it we can sail about and see the originals of the pictures we have been looking at. Large quantities of sponges, turtles, and fish are sent out from Key West to our Atlantic cities. But wrecking is the principal business of the place."

"Why, what does 'wrecking' mean, uncle?" asked Ned.

"You know what we mean when we say a vessel has been wrecked. Don't you?" his uncle asked in reply. "Well, about forty-five or fifty vessels are wrecked in the course of a year near Key West, and the people of that island help to save the cargoes, doing so in a way to benefit the owners as well as themselves. I am told they derive an annual profit of about two hundred thousand dollars."

"Key West is considered an important military station. Is it not?" asked Gracie.

"Yes, being the key to the Florida Pass and the Gulf of Mexico," replied Harold. "It has a large and safe harbor, which will admit vessels drawing twenty-two feet of water. Fort Taylor, which defends it, is a powerful work."

"Oh, I for one expect to have a good time there!" exclaimed his cousin, Elsie. "We can visit the town and the fort to see what they are like, then come back to this yacht and have a good time here while waiting for the rest of our party."

"Yes, I think we can," assented Dr. Harold. "And now suppose we wrap up and go on deck for a little healthful exercise."

They did so, and all greatly enjoyed their promenade, though Ned soon grew weary enough to be glad to go below again and lie down for a little nap. Grandma and his older sister went with him, and the other children soon followed. And so, Gracie and her new husband were finally left alone together—a state of things by no means disagreeable to either. It was still very early in their honeymoon, and dearly as they loved their mother and the little folks so nearly related to them, they were glad now and then to be left quite to themselves—that they might receive and return tokens of their ardent affection unabashed by the thought of indifferent or amused spectators of the scene.

But at length, they began taking note of the progress they were making toward their anchoring destination, and Gracie asked, "How soon do you think we will reach Key West, Harold?"

"I believe that we are nearing it now," replied Harold. "We will anchor in it's harbor tonight, I think."

"Oh, I am glad to hear that!" exclaimed Gracie. "And how soon do you think father and his party will join us?"

"Doubtless in a few days we shall see them. They will come down by rail to Cedar Keys and from there by steamer to Key West."

"They will want to stay a few days to see the sponge auctions, sponge yard, and so forth, too. After that, we will have the rest of our pleasant journey in the yacht to Viamede, mother's beautiful and delightful southern home."

"To me it is both beautiful and delightful," returned Harold, smiling fondly upon her, "and I am very glad that it is so to my little wife also."

"Oh, she's not so very little!" exclaimed Gracie with an amused and happy laugh, drawing herself up to her full height as she spoke.

"Yet rather small compared to her tall and broad-shouldered husband," returned Harold, accompanying his words with a fond caress.

"Now, Rory, leave off, sir;
You'll hug me no more;
That is eight times today
That you've kissed me before,"

sang Gracie, ending with a merry laugh.

"Then here goes another on that to make sure,
For there's luck in odd numbers
says Rory O'More."

rejoined Harold in laughing reply, suiting the action to the word.

The *Dolphin* entered the harbor of Key West early that evening and anchored near the shore.

All her passengers were on deck and were eager to take a bird's eye view of the place, expecting to do more than that in the morning.

"I suppose we will all go ashore directly, or at least pretty soon after breakfast. Won't we, Harold?" asked Elsie Dinsmore.

"Hardly all of us, Cousin Elsie," replied Harold, giving Ned a regretful glance as he spoke. "The exertion would be too great for my young patient's strength, and surely some one of us should stay here in our yacht with him."

"And his grandmother is the very one to do that," quickly responded Mrs. Elsie Travilla.

"But, mother, you should not be deprived of the sight of this town of Key West," remonstrated Harold, and Ned's sisters, Gracie and Elsie, each promptly offered to stay and care for their little invalid brother. "It is very good and kind of you both," remarked Harold with a pleased smile, "but now that I think of it, we are likely to lie in this port for some days. That being the case, we can divide forces and make two trips to the town with some going today, others tomorrow."

"That entirely obviates the difficulty," said his mother. "I will be caretaker of my little grandson today, and perhaps someone else may be tomorrow so that I may take a look around."

A sailor had been sent ashore to inquire for mail and telegrams, and he now approached the party with several letters and a telegram. That last was directed to Dr. Harold, who took and promptly opened it.

"Ah ha!" he said with a pleased smile. "The rest of our party will be here with us soon—tonight or tomorrow, I think."

"Oh, that's good!" cried Ned joyously. "How glad I'll be to see dear papa and mamma! With them here I sha'n't care at all for not being able to go on shore."

Everybody else seemed to share his delight at the prospect of the expected addition to their company and talked merrily of what they hoped to do and see in the next few days.

"I wish you could go ashore with the rest of us, Neddie dear," said his sister in a regretful tone, taking his hand in hers and giving it an affectionate squeeze. "You poor little brother, it does seem hard that you have to miss so many of the pleasures the rest of us have."

"It's good of you to feel so for me, Elsie dear," he replied, returning the squeeze and smiling up into her face, "but I don't mind it a bit if I can have grandma or mamma or papa with me. They're so kind and tell me such nice stories, and I can have a rest or a nap whenever I need it."

CHAPTER EIGHTH

THE DEPARTURE OF the bridal party from Woodburn was soon followed by that of the guests until all were gone but those from Sunnyside. They were entreated to linger and assured there was nothing to hurry them away from their father's house.

"I can't bear to have you go yet," said Violet entreatingly. "You are the only ones of my husband's children left to us, and the house will seem desolate enough to him and me until we, too, can start for Viamede. Besides, none of you are going there with us, so we want to see all we can of you now and here."

"We do, indeed," said the captain. "Especially you, Max, as there is no knowing how long it may be before Uncle Sam will let us have you with us again."

"True, father, and I don't want to lose a minute of the time I may have with you," returned Max feelingly, "or with the other dear ones—wife, sister, and brother," he added, glancing from one to another.

"No, and we all want to be together while we can. It is so sad to have to part even for a time," sighed Lucilla, turning a regretfully affectionate look upon one and another, especially her father, her eyes filling as they met the tenderly loving expression in his.

"Yes, parting is hard," he said with forced cheerfulness, "but we will console ourselves with the thought that it is not likely to be for very long. We seem to be in that respect an usually happy family."

"True, and I think our wedding party has been an entire success," said Violet in her usual sprightly tones. "Nothing went wrong, and our darling Gracie made the loveliest of brides."

There was a word of cordial assent to that from all present except baby Mary, who had fallen asleep in her mother's arms.

"How long may you stay with us this time, Max?" asked Chester.

"I must leave next Tuesday morning," was the reply. "May I trust you to take good care of my wife and daughter while they are left alone with you and Lu?"

"Certainly. I intend to do the very best I can for them," returned Chester with the air of one making a very solemn promise. "I hope you are willing to trust me, Eva?" turning to her.

"Perfectly," she said with a pleasant little laugh. "And Lu and I will try to take good care of baby Mary's Uncle Chester."

"Ah, it seems it is worth my while to claim to be that," he laughed.

"My dear," said Violet, addressing the captain, "don't you think we can make our arrangements to leave for Viamede by next Tuesday morning?"

"Yes, I think we can if you wish to go then," he replied. "By so doing, we should probably reach Key West only a day or two later than our party on the *Dolphin*."

"Which would be very pleasant for our dear ones, especially Elsie and Ned."

"And how glad they will be to see their papa and mamma," remarked Lucilla, unable to repress a small sigh as she spoke.

"Daughter dear, I am sorry, indeed, that you, Chester, Eva, and Max are not all to be of our party," her father said, regarding her with a loving, regretful look. "But cheer up with the thought that the separation is not likely to be a very long one. We may hope to be all together again in a few months, and I hope with Ned quite restored to wonted health and strength."

"Oh, I hope so," she said. "Dear little fellow! His sister is very fond of him. And, father, you will write frequently to me?"

"Every day if you will do the same by me," he answered with a smile. "And in addition to that, we can have telegrams and telephone messages. So, the separation will not be so bad as it was in the days when I was in Uncle Sam's naval service. Now I think I'll go to the telephone and ask if cousins Ronald and Annis can be ready to start on Tuesday morning."

He did so, and the answer came back in the affirmative. Everybody was glad, for those cousins were esteemed good company by one and all, and Ned was known to be always greatly entertained by Cousin Ronald's use of his ventriloquial powers.

"The fun he will make for our Neddie boy will do the little chap a world of good, no doubt," said Max with satisfaction.

"Surely it will," said Lucilla, "and I am so glad that Harold still has him in his charge. Certainly Harold is a skillful physician, even though he is related to us," she added with a little laugh.

"Yes," said her father. "I am glad he is to be with us and that our dear ones here will still have the services of his brother Herbert and Dr. Arthur Conley, who are both equally skillful in the practice of their profession. Don't let them neglect you, daughter," he added earnestly. "Don't fail to summon them promptly, Chester, should any one of you be at all ill."

"Rest assured I will not, sir," returned Chester with prompt decision. "Trust me to do my very best for the health and happiness of the two dear ladies left in my charge and the little newcomer as well."

"Thank you, Chester," said Max. "It is a great comfort to me that I can leave my dear ones in your care."

"It seems hard to give our dear ones into the care of others," sighed Violet. "It was hard for us to part with our darling Neddie for even a few days, but mamma and Harold can and will take better care of him than we could, and we hope to join them very soon."

"Yes," said the captain, "and when we start we may hope to overtake them in somewhat less than two days."

"Yes, father," responded Max. "What a great blessing it is that traveling is so much speedier work than it used to be even not so very many years ago."

"And that messages can be sent and received so promptly by telegraph and the telephone," responded the captain. "It seems to bring distant parts of the world much closer than they used to be, and temporary separations by land or sea are not now the sore trials they were in former days."

"Eva and I feel it a great comfort," said Max, turning to his wife and child with a tender smile. "In case I were needed here, I might be easily summoned and come promptly, even at the risk of having to resign from the navy," he added in a jesting tone.

"Ah, Max, the possibility of tempting you to do so rash an act as that would certainly make me hesitate to summon you, except in a case of the direst necessity," said Eva in tones tremulous with obvious emotion.

"But we will hope that no such necessity may ever arise," remarked Captain Raymond in a cheery tone. "Let us take another look at Gracie's bridal gifts. Many of the gifts are worth some very close scrutiny."

"Yes, indeed," said Violet. "I must see them carefully packed away today or tomorrow."

"Oh, let us help you with it today, Mamma Vi," said Lucilla.

"Thank you, I will," replied Violet.

Examining, chatting over, and the packing away of the numerous bridal gifts occupied the greater part of the afternoon. An early tea followed, and soon after that the Sunnyside folk returned to their homes, thinking it not well to have the baby out any later than that in the cold weather.

For the next few days Violet and the captain felt it lonely enough without the dear ones aboard the *Dolphin*, but they busied themselves with preparations for following them. In the meantime, they greatly enjoyed their daily interaction with their near and loved neighbors—his older children and their baby granddaughter.

So the time passed, and to most of them it seemed but a little while before Tuesday morning dawned. Good-byes were then said. Max went his way northward, and the others of the captain's party took a southbound train of cars, which carried them to Cedar Keys on the western Florida Coast. From there, they went down by steamer to Key West. The captain had sent a telegram ahead, and their arrival was a glad event but not a surprise to the *Dolphin's* passengers. Ned's joy was very great. He had been happy with grandma, uncle, sisters, and cousins, but papa and mamma were even more to him than were they, so that their coming seemed to quicken his recovery. Several days were spent at that port that all might have abundant opportunity to see all on both land and water that they cared to see. Ned had no desire to visit the sponge yards or auctions, but some sponges were brought on board the *Dolphin*. He was rather startled for a moment when, on picking one up, a scream as of pain and anger seemed to come from it. "Don't, you naughty boy! You just let me alone!"

"Oh," cried Ned, dropping it hastily, "I didn't know you were alive. But don't be scared. I'll not hurt you."

Then noticing a quizzical look in his father's eye and catching the sound of a half-smothered laugh from his sister and some of the others, he suddenly comprehended how it happened that the sponge seemed so alive and able to speak in good, plain English.

"Oh, I know. It was Cousin Ronald making the thing talk. For it can't be that it's alive after being pulled up out of the water and scraped and cleaned and all that."

"Silly boy! Dead folks can't talk, but I can," the sponge seemed to reply in a sneering tone.

"No," laughed Ned, "but Cousin Ronald isn't dead, even if you are. Besides, I don't believe you could talk when you were alive."

"Huh? Much you know about it. Some silly little folks think they know a great deal more than they do."

Ned seemed highly amused. "Oh, it's good fun, Cousin Ronald, so please keep it on," he begged, looking up into the kindly face of the beloved old gentleman.

"Well, now," Mr. Lilburn exclaimed, as if much surprised, "I don't live in that bit of sponge."

"No," laughed Ned, "it's much too little for anybody to live in. But I think your voice can get in it, and it's real fun to hear it talk. So, please make it say something more."

"I used to live on the rocks away down under the water," the sponge seemed to say. "That was my home, and I wanted to stay there. But a cruel man came down, pulled me off, and brought me up, and I've had an awful time ever since. They shook me and scraped me and squeezed me so hard and long that now I'm certainly more dead than alive."

"Oh, it's too bad!" exclaimed Ned. "I think they might have let you live on in your own home. Maybe we might send you back to it, if you were alive, but it's no use now if you are dead."

"Well, Neddie boy, don't you think Mr. Sponge has talked enough now?" asked Cousin Ronald in his own natural voice. "I am really afraid our good friends here must be tired of the very sound of his voice."

"Perhaps they are," replied Ned, "and I'm afraid you are tired making him talk. But it has been good fun, and I am very much obliged to you for it, Cousin Ronald."

"You are very welcome," replied Mr. Lilburn. "I'm very glad to give a bit of amusement to a young cousin who has been so ill."

"Thank you, sir. You are always so kind," returned Ned in grateful tones.

All this happened on deck one day late in the afternoon, and Dr. Harold now said he thought it time for his little patient to be taken down into the salon, as the air was growing quite cool.

"Oh, uncle, I don't want to go down to the salon yet, having all this good company," exclaimed Ned imploringly.

"But you don't want to get worse. Do you?" asked Harold in kindly tones.

"And mother will go with you," said Violet, rising and taking his hand in hers.

"Father, too, and he'll carry you down," added the captain, taking the little fellow in his arms and hastening toward the stairway leading to the cabin of the vessel. Violet followed close behind them, and Dr. Harold and Gracie brought up the rear. Grandma Elsie, the younger Elsies, and Alie Leland following them also, and Annis and Cousin Ronald came, too. So, in a few minutes the *Dolphin's* passengers had all deserted the deck for the salon.

Then presently came the call to supper, and all gathered about a table well furnished with wholesome, satisfying food and drink.

Gracie sat at her father's right hand, between him and her husband, and as he carved the fowl and filled the plates, he every now and then gave her a pleased, scrutinizing, smiling glance.

"You are looking bright and well, daughter," he said at length. "Your honeymoon seems to agree with you, though it is perhaps rather early to judge of that."

"It has been delightful so far, papa," she returned with a smiling glance first at him and then up into Harold's face. "It could hardly be otherwise in such a vessel and in such company—with a dear mother, a good doctor, a kind husband—indeed, everything my heart could wish, except the dear ones left behind like my dear father, mamma, and sisters Lu and Eva, not to mention darling baby Mary. And now," she concluded, "since two of my dearest ones and Cousin Ronald and Annis have joined us, I am full of content, of joy, and I am very happy."

"Yes, Gracie, it's ever so nice to have them here—particularly papa and mamma," remarked Ned with a sigh of content. "I hope Cousin Ronald is going to make lots of fun for us."

"But maybe Dr. Harold won't approve of so much fun for his young patient," suggested a voice that seemed to come from somewhere in Ned's rear.

"Oh, who are you now?" queried the little fellow, turning half around in his chair to look behind him.

"Somebody that knows a thing or two," replied the same voice, now apparently coming from a distant part of the room.

"Oh, you do. Do you?" laughed Ned. "Well, I think I begin to know who you are," he added, turning a half-convinced, half-inquiring look upon Cousin Ronald.

"Ha! Ha! Some little boys think themselves very wise, even when they don't understand a matter at all," returned the voice of the ever invisible speaker.

"But I do, though," returned Ned. "I know Cousin Ronald and a thing or two about what he can do. But it's fun, anyhow. It seems so real, even if I do know he's doing it."

"And you think I'm your Cousin Ronald. Do you? Do I look like that old gent?" asked the voice, seeming to come from behind them within an adjoining stateroom.

"Old gent isn't a nice name to give a real gentleman like our Cousin Ronald," retorted Ned in a tone of disgust, which caused a laugh of amusement from most of those about the table.

"There, my son, that will do now. Let us see you finish your supper quietly," said Captain Raymond, and Ned obeyed.

CHAPTER NINTH

THE NEXT MORNING, the weather was such as made the *Dolphin's* salon a far more attractive place to her passengers than was her deck. So there they all gathered and sat chatting cozily together until at length the children began asking Grandma Elsie for another round of her interesting historical stories.

"I think it is Captain Raymond's turn to be narrator now," she said with a smiling glance at him. "I feel inclined to be one of the audience."

"And I am inclined to be a listener to a story from you, mother," he returned pleasantly, "or if you are unwilling to entertain us in that way this morning, perhaps Cousin Ronald may feel inclined to do so."

"Thanks for the invitation, captain, but I would vastly prefer the role of listener," was Mr. Lilburn's response to that.

After a moment's silent consideration, the captain said, "As we are now passing through the Gulf of Mexico, some distance south of the states of Alabama and Mississippi, I suppose a few passages from their history may prove an interesting subject to the younger members of the audience. Shall I give them?"

The query seemed addressed to the children, and it was promptly replied to with a chorus of expressions of pleasure in the prospect. All these knew the captain to be an interesting narrator of historical events.

"I shall begin with Alabama, as it is now the nearer of the two states," he said. "The word Alabama signifies 'Here we rest.' It is an Indian expression. Fernando de Soto was the first white man who ever entered the state. That was in 1540. His coming displeased the Indians who lived there and considered the country their own, therefore they opposed his progress in several battles. He found the Indians there more civilized than in other sections of America, which he visited. Just above the confluence of the Tombigbee and Alabama rivers, they had a place called Maubila, consisting of eighty handsome houses—each one large enough to contain a thousand men. Round about them was a high wall made of immense trunks of trees set deep in the ground and close together and strengthened with cross-timbers and interwoven with large vines.

"De Soto and his men entered the town, and they were presently treacherously attacked by ten thousand Indians. The Spaniards resisted the attack, and a battle ensued that lasted nine hours and resulted in the destruction of the town and the killing of six thousand Indians. The Spaniards, too, suffered terribly, lost eighty men, forty-five horses, and all their baggage and camp equipage."

"So it was very bad for both armies. Wasn't it, papa?" said Ned.

"Yes, it was, indeed," replied his father, "but the Spaniards were the ones most to blame. This country belonged to the Indians. What right had the Spaniards to come here and try to take it from them? Surely, none at all. What presumption it was in the sovereigns of Europe to give to whomever they pleased great tracts of land in America to which they themselves had no real right.

"But to go back to my story. The Indians were desperate, and they fought the invaders, contesting every rood of ground from the hour of their landing. And naturally, whenever a Spaniard fell into their hands, they returned cruelty for cruelty. The Spaniards were very, very cruel to men, women, and children, but de Soto grew tired of having the cruelty of his men returned upon them. Therefore, he invited a powerful Creek chief to meet him for a friendly talk. But the chief scorned the invitation, called the white men by the names they deserved, and gave them warning that he would never cease making war upon them as long as one of their hated race remained in the country. Both he and his followers carried out their threat, resorting to ambush and stealthy surprises, killing scores, whose heads they chopped off and carried on the ends of poles.

"But some of you have been told this story before in our talks over the history of Florida.

"De Soto crossed Northern Georgia and Northeastern Alabama to Maubila, where they had that terrific fight of which I have just told you. The following winter was a severe one passed by the Spaniards in the country of the Chickasaws around the tributaries of the Yazoo. In the spring, a furious engagement took place with the Chickasaws, in which the Spaniards came near being annihilated. In April, the forlorn remnant again began tramping through the wilderness, blindly groping for the land where de Soto had been told he would find great quantities of gold.

"In the month of May in 1541, de Soto and his men reached the bank of the Mississippi River above the mouth of the St. Francis. The men stood a long time, gazing upon it with awe and admiration, for it is one of the mightiest rivers of the world, and they were the first Europeans to see it at any distance above its mouth."

"And did they stop there, papa?" asked Ned.

"No, my son. They were not yet ready to give up their search for gold and for the Pacific Ocean, which they believed was now not far away."

"Didn't know much about geography. Did they?" laughed Ned.

"No, they knew scarcely nothing of the geography of this continent," replied his father. "But perhaps my little son is not much wiser now in regard to what was then the condition of what is now this great country of ours. Can you tell him, Gracie, what it was at that time?"

"In 1540, papa? A wilderness peopled only by Indians and wild beasts. It was not until 1620 that the pilgrims came to Massachusetts. The first settlement in Maryland was not made until 1631. Virginia's first settlers came in 1607. But the French Huguenots planted a colony in South Carolina as early as May of 1562, only twenty years later than de Soto's visit to Alabama. Georgia was the last settled of the thirteen original colonies."

"And those thirteen colonies were all there was of our country at the time of the Revolutionary War. Weren't they?" asked Elsie Dinsmore.

"Yes," replied the captain, "thirteen colonies at the beginning of that war, thirteen states before it ended at last.

"But to go back to the story of Alabama. It seems to have been left to the Indians until the spring of 1682, when Robert Cavalier de la Salle descended the Mississippi to its mouth, named the country Louisiana, and took possession of it in the name of the King of France. All the Mississippi valley was then claimed for France, but in 1763, she ceded it to England. West Florida, from 1764 to 1781, included a good deal of the present territory of Alabama and Mississippi. In May of 1779, Spain declared war against Great Britain, and the next March, the Spanish governor of Louisiana captured Mobile. In 1783, Great Britain ceded to the United States all territory east of the Mississippi, except Florida, which she ceded back to Spain.

"Alabama was at that time almost entirely in the occupation of the Indians. There was a garrison of troops at Mobile, one at St. Stephen's on the Tombigbee, and there were trading posts at different points in the South and West. And now, the United States bought the whole country west of what is now Georgia to the Mississippi. In 1817, it was made the Mississippi Territory. Fort Stoddard was built near the confluence of the Alabama and Tombigbee. During the War of 1812 with Great Britain, there was a great deal of fighting with the Indians of Alabama. The Creeks were the principal tribe, and in 1812, they were stirred up to war by Tecumseh, the celebrated Shawnee warrior. In August, they attacked Fort Mimms. The garrison made a desperate resistance, but they were overcome, and out of three hundred men, women, and children, only seventeen survived the massacre.

"This aroused the adjoining states to action. Generals Jackson, Claiborn, Floyd, and Coffee entered the Indian country and defeated the Indians at Talladega, where 290 of their warriors were slain. In the month of November, General Floyd attacked the Creeks on their sacred ground at Autossee. Four hundred of their houses were burned, and two hundred of their warriors were killed. Among the dead were the kings of Autossee and Tallahassee. The last stand of the Creeks was at Horseshoe Bend, where the Indians fought desperately but were defeated with the loss of nearly six hundred men. The remaining warriors submitted, and in 1814, a treaty of peace was made. The remainder of the Creeks have moved beyond the Mississippi.

"After that, people poured in from Georgia, the two Carolinas, Kentucky, Tennessee, and Virginia. The state grew rapidly in wealth and population, so that in 1860, it was the fourth in the South in importance and the second in the amount of cotton produced."

"It was a slave state. Wasn't it, papa, and one that seceded in the time of the Civil War?" asked Elsie Raymond.

"Yes, on the eleventh of January in 1861, the state seceded from the Union and joined the Southern Confederacy. It was a sad thing for her, for a great deal of the desperate fighting took place within her borders. The losses in the upper counties were immense, and raiding parties frequently desolated the central ones. Forts Gaines and Morgan, defending the entrance to Mobile Bay, were besieged and taken by the United States forces in 1865. In the same year, the victory of Mobile Bay, the severest naval battle of the war, was won by the Union forces under Admiral Farragut."

"But the folks there are not rebs any more, I suppose," remarked Ned in a tone of inquiry.

"No, my son," replied the captain. "I believe that most, if not all, of them are good, loyal people, who are now very proud and fond of this great country, the United States of America."

CHAPTER TENTH

"YOUR STORY OF Alabama was interesting, I think, papa," said Elsie Raymond, "If you are not too tired, won't you now tell us about the Mississippi River?"

"Yes," replied the captain. "I have told you about de Soto and his men coming there in 1540. At that time, what is now the territory of that state was divided between the Chickasaw, Choctaw, and Natchez Indians. It was more than a hundred years afterward in 1681, that la Salle descended the Mississippi River from the Illinois country to the Gulf of Mexico. In 1700, Iberville, the French governor of Louisiana, planted a colony on Ship Island on the gulf coast. That settlement was afterward removed to Biloxi on the mainland. Bienville, another governor of Louisiana, established a post on the Mississippi River and called it Fort Rosalie. It was in 1761, and now the city of Natchez occupies that spot. A few years later in 1729, the Natchez Indians, growing alarmed at the increasing power of the French, resolved to exterminate them. On the twenty-eighth of November of that year, they attacked the settlement of Fort Rosalie and killed the garrison and settlers—seven hundred persons. When that terrible news reached New Orleans, Bienville resolved to retaliate upon the murderers. The Chickasaws were enemies of the Natchez. He applied to them for help, and they furnished him with sixteen thousand warriors. With them and his own troops, Bienville besieged the Natchez in their fort, but they escaped in the night and fled west of the Mississippi. The French followed and forced them to surrender and took them to New Orleans. From there, he sent them to the island of St. Domingo and sold them as slaves."

"All of them, papa?" asked Ned.

"Nearly all, I believe," replied his father. "They were but a small nation, and very little was heard of them after that. The Chickasaws were a large and powerful tribe living in the fertile region of the upper Tombigbee. The French knew that they had incited the Natchez against them, and now Bienville resolved to attack them. In 1736, he sailed from New Orleans to Mobile with a strong force of French troops and twelve hundred Choctaw warriors. From Mobile, he ascended the Tombigbee River in boats for five hundred miles to the southeastern border of the present county of Pontotoc. The Chickasaw fort was a powerful stronghold about twenty-five miles from that point.

"Bienville took measures to secure his boats then advanced against the enemy. He made a determined assault on their fort, but he was repulsed with the loss of one hundred men, which so discouraged him that he dismissed the Choctaws with presents, threw his cannon into the Tombigbee, re-embarked in his boats, floated down the river to Mobile, and from there returned to New Orleans.

"He had expected to have the cooperation of a force of French and Indians from Canada commanded by D'Artaguette, the pride and flower of the French at the North and some Indians from Canada assisted by the Illinois chief Chicago from the shore of Lake Michigan. All these came down the river unobserved to the last Chickasaw bluff. From there, they penetrated into the heart of the country. They encamped near the appointed place of rendezvous with the force of Bienville, and there they waited for intelligence from him. It did not come, and the Indian allies of D'Artaguette became so impatient for war and plunder that they could not be restrained. At length he—D'Artaguette—consented to lead them to the attack. He drove the Chickasaws from two of their fortified villages, but he was severely wounded in his attack on the third. Then the Indians fled precipitately, leaving their wounded commander weltering in his blood. Vincennes, his lieutenant, and their spiritual guide and friend, the Jesuit Senate, refused to fly and shared the captivity of their gallant leader.

"Did the Indians kill them, papa?" asked Ned.

"No, not then, hoping to receive a great ransom for them from Bienville, who was then advancing into their country. They treated them with great care and attention, but when Bienville retreated, they gave up the hope of getting anything for their prisoners and put them to a horrible death, burning them over a slow fire, leaving only one alive to tell of the dreadful fate of their fellow countrymen."

"Oh, how dreadful!" sighed Elsie Raymond. "I'm thankful we did not live in those times and places, papa."

"Yes, so am I," said her father. "God has been very good to us to give us our lives in this good land and these good times. It is years now since the Indians were driven out of Alabama and Mississippi. They and Florida passed into the hands of the English in 1763. In 1783, the country north of the thirty-first parallel was included within the limits of the United States. According to the charter of Georgia, its territory extended to the Mississippi, but in 1795, the legislature of that state sold to the general government the part which now constitutes the states of Alabama and Mississippi. In 1798, the Territory of Mississippi was organized, and on the tenth of December in 1817, it was admitted into the Union as a state. On the ninth of January in 1861, the state seceded from the Union and joined the Southern Confederacy. Some dreadful battles were fought there in our Civil War—those of Iuka and Corinth, Jackson, Champion Hills, and other places. That war caused an immense destruction of property. The state was subject to military rule until the close of the year 1869, when it was readmitted into the Union."

The captain paused, seeming to consider his story of the settlement of the state of Mississippi completed, but Grandma Elsie presently asked, "Isn't there something more of interest in the story of the Natchez you could tell us, captain?"

"Perhaps so, mother," he replied. "They were a remarkable tribe, more civilized than any other of the original inhabitants of these states. Their religion was something like that of the fire-worshippers of Persia. They called their chiefs 'suns' and the king the 'Great Sun.' A perpetual fire was kept burning by the ministering priest in the principal temple, and he also offered sacrifices of the first fruits of the chase. In extreme cases, when they deemed their deity angry with them, they offered sacrifices of their infant children to appease his wrath. When Iberville was there, one of the temples was struck by lightning and set on fire. The keeper of the flame begged the squaws to throw their little ones into the fire to appease the angry god, and four little ones were so sacrificed before the French could persuade them to desist from the horrid rite. The 'Great Sun,' as they called their king, had given Iberville a hearty welcome to his dominions, paying him a visit in person. He was borne to Iberville's quarters on the shoulders of some of his men and attended by a great retinue of his people. A treaty of friendship was made, and the French given permission to build a fort and establish a trading-post among the Indians—things that, however, were not done for many years. A few stragglers at that time took up their abode among the Natchez, but it was not until 1716 that any regular settlement was made. Then Fort Rosalie was erected at that spot on the banks of the Mississippi where the city of Natchez now stands.

"Well, as I have told you, Grand or Great Sun, the chief of the Natchez, was at first the friend of the whites. But one man, by his overbearing behavior, brought destruction on the whole colony. The home of the Great Sun was a beautiful village called the White Apple. It was spread over a space of nearly three miles, and it stood about twelve miles south of the fort near the mouth of Second Creek, three miles east of the Mississippi. M. D. Chopart, the commander of the fort, was so cruel and overbearing and so unjust to the Indians, that he commanded the Great Sun to leave the village of his ancestors because he, M. D. Chopart, wanted the grounds for his own purposes. Of course, the Great Sun was not willing, but Chopart was deaf to all his entreaties, which led the Natchez to form a lot to rid their country of these oppressors.

"Before the attempt to carry it out, a young Indian girl, who loved the Sieur de Mace, ensign of the garrison, told him with tears that her nation intended to massacre the French. He was astonished and questioned her closely. She gave him simple answers, shedding tears as she spoke, and he was convinced that she was telling him only the truth. So he at once reported it to Chopart, but he immediately had the young man arrested for giving a false alarm.

"But the fatal day came on November the twenty-ninth of 1729. Early in the morning, Great Sun with a few chosen warriors, who were all well armed with knives and other concealed weapons, went to Fort Rosalie. Only a short time before, the company had sent up a large supply of powder, lead, and provisions for the fort. The Indians had brought corn and poultry to barter for ammunition, saying they wanted it for a great hunt they were preparing for, and the garrison, believing their story, were thrown off their guard. They allowed a number of the Indians to come into their fort, while others were distributed about the company's warehouse. Then, after a little while, the Great Sun gave the signal, and the Indians at once drew out their weapons and began a furious massacre of the garrison and all who were in or near the warehouse. The same bloody work was carried on in the houses of the settlers outside the fort.

"It was at nine o'clock in the morning that the dreadful slaughter began, and before noon the whole male population of that French colony— seven hundred souls—were sleeping the sleep of death. The women and children were kept as prisoners, and the slaves that they might be of use as servants. Also two mechanics, a tailor and a carpenter, were permitted to live, that they might be of use to their captors. Chopart was one of the first killed—by a common Indian, as the chiefs so despised him that they disdained to even soil their hands with his blood.

"The Great Sun sat in the warehouse while the massacre was going on, smoking his pipe unconcernedly while his warriors were piling up the heads of the murdered Frenchmen in a pyramid at his feet with Chopart's head at its top, above all those of his officers and soldiers. As soon as the Great Sun had been told by his Indians that all the Frenchmen were dead, he bade them begin their pillage. They then made the slaves bring out the plunder for distribution, except the powder and military stores, which were kept for public use in future emergencies."

"And did they bury all those seven hundred folks they had killed, papa?" asked Ned.

"No," replied his father, "they left them lying strewed about in every place where they had struck them down to death, dancing over their mangled bodies with horrid yells in their drunken revelry. They left them there unburied, as prey for hungry dogs and vultures, and all the dwellings in all the settlements they burned to ashes."

"Didn't anybody at all get away from them, uncle?" asked Alie Leland.

"Nobody who was in the buildings at the time of the massacre," replied the captain. "But two soldiers who happened to be then in the woods escaped and carried the dreadful tidings back to New Orleans."

"I'm glad they didn't go back to the fort and get caught by those savage Indians," said Elsie Dinsmore. "How did they know that the Indians were there and doing such dreadful deeds?"

"By hearing the deafening yells of the savages and seeing the smoke going up from the burning buildings. Those things told them what was going on, and they hid themselves until they could get a boat or canoe in which to go down the river to New Orleans, which they reached in a few days. There, as I have said, they told the sad story of the awful happenings at the colony on the St. Catherine."

"Were there any other colonies that the Indians destroyed in that part of our country, papa?" asked his daughter Elsie.

"Yes, one on the Yazoo near Fort St. Peter, and those on the Washita at Sicily Island and near the present town of Monroe. It was a sad time for every settlement in the province.

"When the news of this terrible disaster reached New Orleans, the French began a war of extermination against the Natchez. They drove them across the Mississippi and finally scattered and extirpated them. The Great Sun and his war chiefs were taken, shipped to St. Domingo, and sold as slaves. Some of the poor wretches were treated with barbaric cruelty—four men and two women were publicly burned to death at New Orleans. Some Tonica Indians brought down a Natchez woman, whom they had found in the woods, and were allowed to burn her to death on a platform erected near the levee, the whole population looking on while she was consumed by the flames. She bore all that torture with wonderful fortitude, not shedding a tear but upbraiding her torturers with their want of skill, flinging at them every epithet she could think of."

"How very brave she must have been, poor thing!" remarked Gracie. "Papa, have not the Natchez always been considered superior to other tribes in refinement and intelligence?"

"Yes," he replied, "it is said that no other tribe has left so proud a memorial of their courage, independent spirit, and contempt of death in defense of their rights and liberties. The scattered remnants of the tribe sought an asylum among the Chickasaws and other tribes who were hostile to the French. But since that time, the individuality of the Natchez tribe has been swallowed up among others with whom they incorporated. In refinement and intelligence they were equal, if not superior, to any other tribe north of Mexico. In courage and stratagem, they were inferior to none. Their form was noble and commanding, their persons were straight and athletic, their stature seldom under six feet. Their countenance indicated more intelligence than is commonly found. Some few individuals of the Natchez tribe were to be found in the town of Natchez as late as the year 1782, more than half a century after the Natchez massacre."

CHAPTER ELEVENTH

"WELL, WELL, WELL! I should think you youngsters might be ashamed to keep the poor captain talking and telling stories so long, just for your amusement," remarked a strange voice, coming apparently from the half open doorway of a nearby stateroom. "Can't you let him have a little rest now?"

"Of course," replied Ned. "He tells splendid stories, and we like to listen to them. But we don't want him to go on if he feels tired, for he is our own dear, kind, good papa, whom we love ever so much."

"Huh!" returned the voice. "Actions speak louder than words. So don't coax for any more stories now. You should have a good game of romps instead."

"The rest can do that," said Ned, "but my uncle doctor wouldn't be likely to let me romp very much."

"And you think you have to obey him. Do you, sonny boy?"

"Of course, if I want him to cure me, and I'm very sure you would think me a naughty boy if I didn't obey."

"If you didn't want to be cured?"

"No, if I didn't mind my doctor."

"I thought he was your brother. He's married to your sister. Isn't he?"

"Yes," laughed Ned, "and that makes him my brother. But he's my mother's own brother, and that makes him my uncle. So he's both uncle and brother, and that makes him a very near relation to me, indeed."

"So it does, my little fellow, and you had better mind all he says, even if he is a young doctor that doesn't know quite all the old doctors do."

"He knows a great deal," cried Ned rather indignantly, "lots more, I guess than some of the other doctors that think they are very smart and know everything."

"Well, you needn't get mad about it," returned the voice. "I like Dr. Harold Travilla, and when I get sick I expect to send for him."

"But who are you?" asked Ned. "Why don't you come out of the stateroom and show yourself?"

"Perhaps I might if I got a polite invitation," replied the voice.

Ned was silent for moment, first looking steadily toward the door from which the voice had seemed to come, then turning a scrutinizing, questioning gaze upon Cousin Ronald.

The others in the room were all watching the two and listening as if much entertained by the talk between them.

"I just know it's you, Cousin Ronald, making fun for us all," the little boy remarked at length.

"That's very kind of you, for fun is right good for folks. Isn't it, Uncle Harold?"

"Yes, I think so," replied the doctor. "'Laugh and grow fat' is an old saying. So I hope the fun will prove beneficial to my young patient."

"I hope so, too," said the captain, "and now suppose you young folks rest yourselves with some sort of games."

"I think we should all wrap up and try a little exercise upon the deck first and after that have some games," said Harold, and everybody promptly followed his advice.

When they had had their exercise and played a few games, dinner was served. After that, they again gathered in the salon, and presently the young folks asked for another of the captain's interesting stories of the states.

"Well, my dears, about which state do you wish to hear now?" he asked.

"I believe we all want Louisiana, papa," replied his daughter Elsie. "We know the story of the battle of New Orleans under General Jackson— that grand victory—and pretty much all that went on in the time of the Civil War, I believe. But I don't remember that you have ever given us any of the early history of that state."

"Well, I shall try to do so now," her father said in reply, and after a moment's silent thought about the subject, he began.

"Louisiana is the central Gulf state of the United States, and it has the Gulf of Mexico for its southern boundary and the Sabine River and

Texas form the western boundary. On the eastern side is the Mississippi River, separating it from the state of that name, which is the northern boundary of that part of Louisiana on the eastern part of the river. The part west of the river is bounded on the north by Arkansas.

"That part of what is now our country was not taken by the whites from the Indians so early as the more northern and eastern parts. History tells us that Robert Cavalier de la Salle descended the Mississippi to its mouth in April of 1682, named the country Louisiana, and took possession of it in the name of the King of France. In 1699, Iberville tried to form a settlement along the lower part of the river, but he succeeded only in forming the colony of Biloxi, in what is now the state of Mississippi. In 1712, Louis XIV of France named the region for himself and granted it to a wealthy capitalist Antony Crozat, giving him exclusive trading rights in Louisiana for ten years. In about half that time, Crozat gave back the grant to the King, complaining that he had not been properly supported by the authorities and had suffered such losses in trying to settle the province as almost to ruin him.

"In the same year, a man named John Law got King Louis to give him a charter for a bank, for a Mississippi company, and to grant the province to them. For a time, he carried out his scheme so successfully that the stock of the bank went up to six hundred times its par value, but it finally exploded and ruined everyone concerned in it.

"It had, however, accomplished the settlement of New Orleans. In 1760, a war was begun between England and France, in which the former took Canada from the latter. Then a good many Canadians emigrated to Louisiana and settled in that part of it west of the Mississippi. In 1762, France ceded her possession in Louisiana west of the Mississippi to Spain, and the country east of that river to England. New Orleans was soon taken possession of by the Spanish authorities, who proved themselves so cruel and oppressive that the French settlers were filled with dismay. The Spaniards still held that province at the time of the American Revolution, and near the close of that war, the Spanish governor of New Orleans captured the British garrison at Baton Rouge."

"I suppose that was hardly because he wanted to help us," laughed Elsie Dinsmore.

"No," smiled the captain, "I rather think he wanted to help himself. The navigation of the Mississippi River was open to all nations by the treaty of 1783, but the New Orleans Spaniards completely neutralized it by seizing all merchandise brought to that city in any but Spanish ships. In 1800, Spain ceded Louisiana back to France, but it suited Napoleon, then emperor of that country, to keep the transfer secret until 1803. He then sent Laussat as prefect of the colony, who informed the people that they were given back to France, which news filled the French settlers with great joy.

"Jefferson was then President, and on learning these facts, he directed Robert Livingston, the American Minister at Paris, to insist upon the free navigation of the Mississippi and to negotiate for the acquisition of New Orleans itself and the surrounding territory. Mr. Monroe was appointed with full powers to assist him in the negotiation.

"Bonaparte acted promptly. He saw that the English wanted Louisiana and the Mississippi River, and he was determined that they should not have them. They had twenty vessels in the Gulf of Mexico, and he saw that they might easily take Louisiana. To deprive them of all prospect of that, he was inclined to cede it to the United States. He—Bonaparte—speedily decided to sell to the United States not New Orleans only, but the whole of Louisiana, and he did so. On the thirtieth of April in 1803, the treaty was signed. Our country was to pay $15,000,000 for the colony, be indemnified for some illegal captures, and the vessels of France and Spain with their merchandise were to be admitted into all ports of Louisiana free of duty for twelve years. Bonaparte stipulated in favor of Louisiana that as soon as possible it should be incorporated into the Union and its inhabitants enjoy the same rights, privileges, and immunities as other citizens of the United States. The third article of the treaty, securing these benefits to them, was drawn up by Bonaparte himself and presented to the plenipotentiaries with the request that they would make it known to the people of Louisiana that the French regretted to part with them and had stipulated for all the advantages they could desire. He also wanted them to know that in giving them up, France had secured them the greatest of all. For, in becoming independent, they would prosper as they never could have done under any European government. But he bade them, while enjoying the privileges of liberty, ever to remember that they were French and preserve for their mother country the affection which a common origin inspires.

"This was a most important transaction, and its completion gave equal satisfaction to both parties. Livingston said, 'I consider that from this day the United States takes rank with the first powers of Europe, and she is entirely escaped from the power of England.' Bonaparte said, 'By this cession of territory I have secured the power of the United States and given to England a maritime rival who at some future time will humble her pride.'"

"And that seems like a prophecy that came true, when one thinks of Jackson's victory on the eighth of January in 1815," remarked Grandma Elsie in her pleasant voice.

"Yes," assented the captain, "that was a signal overthrow to all of the British troops on the plains of Louisiana."

"Yes, I remember that was a great victory for our United States troops," said Elsie Dinsmore. "But who of our folks took possession now that it

was bought from the French, and just when did they do it?"

"It was on the twentieth of December of that same year," replied the captain, "that General Wilkinson and Governor Claiborne, who were jointly commissioned to take possession of the territory for the United States, entered New Orleans at the head of the American troops. The French governor gave up his command, and the tri-colored flag of France gave place to the star-spangled banner."

"Oh, that was very good," said Elsie Dinsmore. "Was Louisiana made a state in the Union at once, Captain Raymond?"

"No," he replied. "It was first erected into a Territory by Congress in 1804. In 1810, the Spanish post at Baton Rouge was seized by the United States forces under General Wilkinson, and the territory connected with it added to Louisiana, which in 1812, was admitted into the Union as a state."

"But, papa, was what is now the state of Louisiana all we bought from France by that treaty of 1803?" asked Gracie.

"No, by no means," replied the captain. "The huge territory covering more than 800,000 square miles that was purchased by that important treaty is now occupied by the states of Louisiana, Arkansas, Missouri, Iowa, Minnesota, Kansas, Nebraska, Oregon, the Dakotas, Colorado, Utah, Wyoming, Montana, Idaho, and Washington."

"My, what a big purchase it was!" cried Ned. "But how did France get so much?"

"No doubt she just helped herself," laughed his sister. "That state went out of the Union in the time of the Civil War. Didn't it, papa?"

"Yes, on the twenty-sixth of January in 1861, but she was readmitted into the Union on the twenty-fifth of June in 1868."

❧❦❧❦❧❦❧❦

CHAPTER TWELFTH

"THESE STORIES OF THE states have been very interesting to me, captain," remarked Mr. Lilburn, breaking a little pause that had followed the conclusion of the brief sketch just given of the early history of Louisiana.

"I feel flattered that my crude efforts in that line should be so highly appreciated," returned the captain with a gratified smile as he spoke. Then he added, "Now, if you feel like making a return in kind, Cousin Ronald, suppose you give us a page or two of Scottish history. I think there is hardly anything more interesting."

"I acknowledge that it is very interesting to me, a native of that land, though now feeling myself a full-fledged American, but how is it with these younger folks?" returned Mr. Lilburn, glancing inquiringly around upon the ladies and children there in the salon.

It was Grandma Elsie who answered in tones of pleased anticipation, "Indeed, cousin, I should be delighted. To me, the history of that grandfather land of mine is only secondary in interest to that of this, my dear native land, which is consequently largely peopled by the descendants of those who struggled so bravely for civil and religious liberty in Scotland."

"Ah, cousin mine, I am glad to ken that you care for that auld fatherland o' yours and mine," returned the old gentleman, smiling affectionately upon her. "There are many passages of history that are interesting and heart stirring to the pride and love of the descendants of the actors in the same. But to what particular passage in her history shall I call your attention to now?"

The query seemed addressed to all present, and Elsie Dinsmore answered quickly and earnestly, "Oh, tell us all you can about that beautiful, unfortunate Mary, Queen of Scots. I suppose you must have seen all the palaces and castles she ever lived in there in Scotland?"

"Yes, my bonny bairn, I have, and I regard them with great interest because of her one-time occupation of them. Linlithgow Castle is now only a picturesque old ruin, yet one may stand in the very room, now roofless, to be sure, where Queen Mary was born. The walls of the castle were very thick and strong but not then deemed strong enough to protect the royal infant born on the seventh of December in 1542. There was rejoicing at her birth, but it would have been greater had she been a lad instead of a lass. Her father, then on his deathbed, exclaimed when he heard the news, 'Woe to the crown of Scotland. It came with a lass and it will go with a lass.'

"Her sex was a disappointment to Scottish hearts, yet still they loved her and would do all in their power to protect and defend her, especially from the English King Henry VIII, with whom they were then at war and who was doing all in his power to get possession of the little princess, purposing in time to marry her to his son and so unite the two kingdoms under one crown."

"Why, that would have been a fine way to put a stop to the fighting between the two kingdoms, I should think," said Elsie Dinsmore.

"Perhaps, if he offered good terms, but those he offered were so harsh that Scotland's Parliament rejected them. For greater security, both Mary and her mother were taken from Linlithgow to Stirling Castle, a grand fortress atop of a lofty hill above the peaceful valley of Monteith. It seemed a safe place for the bonny baby queen, but some wicked, treacherous men formed a plot to carry her off to England. It failed because her guardians were so very cautious as never to admit more than one person at a time to see her.

"With so many dangers threatening her, it was thought best to crown her queen as soon as possible, and when she was nine months old, she was one Sunday morning taken from her nursery to the chapel of the castle. There one of her nobles held her on the throne and spoke for her the words she should have spoken had she been old enough. Then the Cardinal held the crown over her head, for a moment clasped her tiny fingers about the scepter, and buckled the sword of state around her waist. Then every peer and prelate present, one after another, knelt before her, held his right hand above her baby head, and swore to defend her with his life. But alas, alas! Few o' them proved faithful to their oath.

"A strange life lay before that little babe. She was perhaps six years of age when taken to France as a safer place for her than Scotland. She was married early in life to the young King Francis II, but in seventeen months his death made her a widow. She left France for her own land and arrived at Leith in August of 1561, doubtless little dreaming the sad fate in store for her in the British Isles," sighed the kind-hearted old gentleman. Then for a moment, he seemed lost in thought.

"Can you tell us in what town and castle she made her home?" asked Elsie Dinsmore.

"Holyrood Castle in Edinburgh," replied Mr. Lilburn. "It was in the chapel of that castle she was married to her cousin, Henry Stuart, the Lord Darnley, in July of 1565. She was then about twenty-three years of age."

"Did she love him, Cousin Ronald?" asked Elsie Raymond.

"No doubt of it, lassie, for she had plenty of other offers. It seemed as though every royal bachelor and widower wanted her for a wife. It is but a small wonder, for she was very beautiful.

"She called Darnley the handsomest man she had ever seen. Doubtless it was his good looks she fell in love with, but a few weeks of wifehood with him showed her that his character was far less admirable than his looks. He was vain, selfish, ungrateful, took all her favors as a matter of course, and asked for more. Soon after their marriage, the English ambassador wrote of them, 'The Queen doth everything in her power to oblige Darnley, but Darnley does not do the least thing to oblige her.' She had a few weeks of happiness during their wedding journey through the interior of Scotland, but soon after that Darnley began treating her with brutal unkindness. At a public banquet, only four months after their marriage, he began to drink to excess, urging his guests to do the same. Queen Mary tried quietly to check him, but he turned upon her with such vulgar violence that she left the room in tears. And he was so insolent to the Court in general that he was soon almost universally detested."

"And I should hardly think it possible for poor Queen Mary to go on loving him," said Elsie Dinsmore quietly.

"Nor should I," said Mr. Lilburn. "Certainly, he was very different from what she had believed him to be when she married him. And, poor lady, she greatly needed the right sort of husband to protect and help her. The nobles who surrounded her were treacherous, unprincipled men, ready to commit any crime that would enable them to govern Scotland to suit themselves, by making the sovereign a mere cipher in their hands. I presume you all know something of the brutal murder of Rizzio?"

"Yes, sir, I believe we do. But please tell us the whole story about it," said Elsie Raymond.

"He was a singer in the chapel of Holyrood Castle and had a voice of wonderful power and sweetness, which so pleased the Queen that she made him leader of the singing in her chapel services. He was a homely man, but he was a clever linguist, faithful and prudent, and Queen Mary made him her private secretary. The treacherous lords wanted to get rid of him because he was not one of them and because he had so great influence with the Queen. They determined to murder him on the pretense that the Queen was so fond of him as to make Darnley jealous. It was all a pretense just to trump up a reason for murdering Rizzio.

"One evening in March in 1566, Queen Mary was in her library at supper with three friends as her guests—a lady, a gentleman, and Rizzio. She did not know that her Lord Chancellor Morton had, just after dusk, led a body of armed men into the courtyard of this, her Holyrood Castle. Some of these men had hidden themselves in Darnley's room, just underneath these apartments of hers, and a winding staircase led up from them. Suddenly Darnley, who had come up this private stairway, entered the room, sat down in a vacant chair beside her, put his arm around her waist, and gave her an affectionate kiss.

"It was a Judas kiss, for at the same time the murderers whom he was assisting had stolen softly into the Queen's bedroom. Now they crowded through the doorway into her presence. She was alarmed and at once demanded the reason for their intrusion.

"They said they meant no harm to her, only to the villain near her.

"Rizzio understood and said to her, 'Madam, I am lost!' 'Fear not,' she answered, 'the King will never suffer you to be slain in my presence, nor can he forget your many faithful services.'

"The words seemed to touch Darnley's heart and made him unwilling to perform his part in the wicked work, and Ruthven exclaimed fiercely, 'Sir, look to your wife and sovereign.'

"At that, Darnley forced Mary into a chair and held her there so tightly that she could not rise, while one of the ruffians presented a pistol to her side and swore a horrible oath that he would shoot her dead if she resisted.

"'Fire,' she replied, 'if you have no respect for my life,' and her husband pushed away the weapon from her head.

"But now others of the murderous crowd were in the room, lighting it up with the glare of torches, and Rizzio, clinging to the Queen's dress, begged piteously, 'Save my life, madam! Save my life for God's dear sake!'

"But she could not. The assassins rushed upon him, overturning the table with its lights and dishes. Queen Mary fainted, and Rizzio was dragged out into a narrow passageway and stabbed again and again until his shrieks were hushed in death. There is still a stain upon

Holyrood's floor said to have been caused by his blood."

"And what about Queen Mary? Did they hurt her, Cousin Ronald?" asked Ned, very much interested in the story.

"When she came out of her faint, poor lady, those lawless nobles, wicked murderers, told her she was their prisoner. They set a guard at her door and left her to spend the night in anxiety, horror, and fear."

"Oh, how wicked and cruel they were!" exclaimed Elsie Raymond. "I hope they got punished for it somehow!"

"It looks as though Darnley did," said Mr. Lilburn. "In a little less than a year after the murder of Rizzio he, having gone with a few friends to a private house, was during the night blown up with gunpowder, and only two months afterward, Queen Mary married the Earl of Bothwell. That disgusted her best subjects, so that they made her a prisoner and forced her to abdicate in favor of her son, James VI.

"Queen Mary escaped from her prison and collected a large army. They fought for the recovery of her crown and throne, but they were defeated. She then fled to England, but Queen Elizabeth, though her cousin, was very jealous of her and kept her imprisoned there for many years. She then had Mary beheaded."

"Had she any right to do that?" asked Elsie Dinsmore in indignant tones.

"No," replied Mr. Lilburn, "none but the might that is said to make right. Queen Mary was in Queen Elizabeth's power with none to defend her. Queen Mary, when on trial, said to her judges, 'I am a Queen, subject to none but God. Him do I call to witness that I am innocent of all the charges brought against me. And recollect, my lords, the theater of the world is wider than the realm of England.'"

"Did they kill her, Cousin Ronald?" asked Ned.

"Yes, they beheaded her in Fotheringay Castle. It is said that every one was impressed by the melancholy sweetness of her face and the remains of her rare beauty as she drew near the spot where her life was to be ended. Her executioners knelt down and asked her forgiveness for what they were about to do, and she replied, 'I forgive you and all the world with all my heart.' Then turning to the women who attended her, she said, 'Pray do not weep. Believe me, I am happy to leave the world. Tell my son that I thought of him in my last moments and that I sincerely hope his life may be happier than mine.'

"Then there was a dreadful silence as she knelt down and laid her head upon the block. In another minute, the chief executioner held it up in his hand saying, 'So perish all enemies of Queen Elizabeth.'"

"What a shame!" cried Ned. "I hope the time came when Queen Elizabeth had to have her head chopped off."

"No," replied Mr. Lilburn, "but hers was not a happy death. She seems to have been almost crazed with grief and remorse over the death of Essex, threw herself on the floor, and lay there refusing food and medicine for several days and nights until death came to end the sorrowful scene at long last."

"Then, perhaps she suffered more than Queen Mary did in her dying time, as I certainly think she deserved to," said Elsie Dinsmore.

"Yes, I think she did," responded Mr. Lilburn. "It seems very possible that her cruel, unjust treatment of her cousin, Queen Mary, may have helped to burden her conscience and increase her remorse till she felt that life was a burden too heavy to bear."

"Do you think she really wanted to die and was courting death, Cousin Ronald?" asked Grandma Elsie.

"Her refusal of food and medicine looks like it," he replied. "Yet one can hardly suppose that death would be anything but a terror to one whose character was so far from Christian. Her public conduct was worthy of the highest encomium, but not so with her private life. Yet I wadna wish to sit in judgment on her at this late day."

CHAPTER THIRTEENTH

THE NEXT DAY was the Sabbath, and the weather was clear and mild enough for all, passengers and crew, to gather upon the deck for a short service of prayer, singing of hymns, and a sermon read by the captain. After that, there was an hour of Bible study in the salon, Mr. Lilburn leading by request of the others.

Turning over the leaves of his Bible, "Suppose we take for our subject the confessing of Christ before men," he said. "Here in Romans we read, 'The word is nigh thee, even in thy mouth, and in thy heart; that is, the word of faith which we preach; that if thou shalt confess with thy mouth the Lord Jesus, and shalt believe in thine heart that God hath raised Him from the dead, thou shalt be saved. For with the heart man believeth unto righteousness; and with the mouth confession is made unto salvation. For the Scripture saith, "Whosoever believeth on Him shall not be ashamed."'

"What a burning desire Paul had for the salvation of souls. He said, 'Brethren, my heart's desire and prayer to God for Israel is that they might be saved.' And if we are Christians we will be often in prayer and often making effort for the salvation of souls. Let us ask ourselves if it is indeed so with us. And let us strive to make it so, earnestly doing all in our power to win souls to Christ, telling them of the great love wherewith He has loved us, bleeding and dying that we might live, and that all we have to do is simply to come, to believe, to take this offered salvation. 'Whosoever shall call upon the name of the Lord shall be saved.' We have only to call upon His name with real desire for His help, and in an instant He is with us, offering us full and free salvation, purchased for us by His suffering and death, so that we may have it without money and without price. Now, friends, please read in turn texts bearing upon this great subject."

Then Grandma Elsie read, "'For God so loved the world, that He gave His only begotten Son that whosoever believeth in Him should not perish, but have everlasting life. For God sent not His Son into the world to condemn the world; but that the world through Him might be saved.'"

Then Gracie, "'Christ is the end of the law for righteousness to everyone that believeth.'"

Then the captain read, "'Knowing that a man is not justified by the works of the law, but by the faith of Jesus Christ, even we have believed in Jesus Christ, that we might be justified by the faith of Christ, and not by the works of the law: for by the law shall no flesh be justified.'"

Then Violet, "'By grace ye are saved through faith; and that not of yourselves; it is the gift of God, not of works, lest any man should boast.'"

Harold was the next, "'God hath not appointed us to wrath, but to obtain salvation by our Lord Jesus Christ,'" he read, and that closed the lesson, the younger ones seeming to have nothing ready. Presently came the summons to the dinner table.

"Aren't we getting pretty near to Louisiana, papa?" asked Ned at the breakfast table the following morning.

"Near enough for a distant view of its shore," was the smiling reply.

"Oh, I'm glad! Are we going to stop at New Orleans, papa?"

"No, we will not go up to that city this time, but we will travel directly to Viamede by the shortest route."

"Oh, I am glad of that, for I just long for a sight of our beautiful Viamede, and I think I shall get well there very fast," laughed Ned.

"Maybe so, if you are careful to obey your doctor," said Harold, smiling kindly upon the little fellow.

"It will be ever so nice to get there," exclaimed Elsie Raymond. "Grandma, you were so kind to invite us all."

"Not kinder to you than to myself, since to have you all there makes the place twice as enjoyable and attractive to me," was the usual pleasant-toned reply.

"Will the friends and relatives about there be expecting us, mother?" asked Gracie.

"I think they will, as they were written to that we expected to arrive just about the time we are now likely to reach there."

"I think we shall," said the captain, and they did find the expectant relatives gathered at the wharf ready to give them a joyful greeting. For dearly they all loved Viamede's sweet mistress, and they also cherished a warm affection for those who accompanied her, especially her son Harold and his bride. The congratulations to them were warm, especially those of Dr. Percival, who felt that he owed his life to God's blessing upon Harold's wise and kind treatment during the severe injury caused by that sad fall from his horse many months ago.

And now he and his Maud had a treasure, which they were very proud to show to Grandma Elsie and all the others—a lovely baby girl, another Elsie. And Dr. and Mrs. Johnson had still another to show, exhibiting her with much parental pride, speaking of her as still another namesake for their dearly loved cousin, Mrs. Elsie Travilla.

She was much moved. "I am greatly honored," she said, "so many naming their darlings for me. I have brought two with me—Elsie Dinsmore and Elsie Raymond. There is another one—Elsie Keith—at the Parsonage and one at Magnolia Hall—Elsie Embury. Now these two dear babies, making six here in all. Yes, and in my more northern home neighborhood there is my eldest daughter, named for me by her father, and there are several others, the children of friends who have honored me in the same way. I certainly am greatly honored. But dear Dick and Bob, will it not make confusion to have two of the same name at Torriswood?"

"Oh, I think not, cousin," laughed Dick. "Ours can be Elsie P. and Bob's Elsie J."

"And, oh, Cousin Elsie, if only they get your sweet disposition along with the name," exclaimed Maud, "they will have reason to thank us for giving it to them."

"As I certainly do my father and mother," said little Elsie Keith, standing near and listening with interest to the talk about the name she bore. "They have often told me I must try to be like the dear lady relation whose name I bear."

"Dear child, may you succeed in greatly improving upon your pattern," Mrs. Travilla responded, smiling upon the little girl, gently smoothing her hair, and giving her a kiss.

But now came the summons to the dinner table. By the written orders of Viamede's mistress sent weeks before, a fine, abundant, luxurious meal had been made ready for the occasion, and soon all were seated about the hospitable board regaling themselves upon all the luxuries to be had in that part of the country at that time of the year.

They ate with good appetites, at the same time enjoying the feast of reason and the flow of the soul.

The children had a table to themselves that they might chatter to their hearts' content without disturbing the older folk, and they fully appreciated the privilege.

"Oh, Elsie Raymond!" exclaimed Mildred Keith, the eldest of the children from the Parsonage. "I haven't seen your tee-tee. Didn't you bring him along?"

"No," replied Elsie. "Ned's couldn't be brought because he was not well enough to care for it on the *Dolphin*, and we wouldn't have felt willing to leave it to other folks to be troubled with. So, they had to be left at home, and as we didn't want to part them, I left mine, too."

"Oh, that was good and kind of you," was Mildred's remark.

"So we won't have the tee-tees to make fun for us with Cousin Ronald's help," said another of the cousins. "But I know he can make fun even without the little monkeys."

"He's always so very kind about making fun for us," said another. "He's a dear old gentleman! I'm as fond of him as if he was a near relation."

"And you had a wedding at your house just a little while ago," said another. "I like both Cousin Harold and Cousin Gracie, and it seems nice that they are married to each other."

"But does Cousin Violet like it? I heard the folks say it would make her mother to her brother."

"Yes, but, besides, it makes mamma and Gracie sisters. So, Gracie can say mamma or sister, just as she pleases, but I don't believe it will make a bit of difference in their love for each other."

"No, I don't believe it will, or make her, your mother, and Dr. Harold feel at all differently toward each other. I daresay they will all feel and act toward each other about as they did before the wedding."

"I'm sorry your sisters Lu and Eva didn't come this time and bring that little Mary. Why didn't they and Chester come?"

"Chester couldn't well leave his business, Sister Lu didn't want to leave him, and Eva thought home was better for baby Mary," Elsie Raymond said in reply. "It seemed hard to leave them behind, but papa said it couldn't be helped. Oh, I wish you could all see baby Mary! She is such a dear, pretty, little thing."

The talk was not all going on at the children's table. The grown folks were doing their full share and that with evident enjoyment.

"We understood, Cousin Elsie," said Dr. Percival, "that the cousins from the Oaks and Fairview were to be here.

"Yes, and I think they will be in a few days, coming by rail. They were not quite ready to start when we were, nor would the yacht have held us all. And we may hope for another gathering when they do get here," she added with a merry look and her musical laugh.

"Ah, that's a pleasant prospect, if we are to be invited to take part in it," laughed the doctor.

"Ah, Dick, you surely know that is, of course," she returned with a look that said more than her words. "A family party here without you in it would hardly be worthy of that name to me."

"Ah, cousin, you are indeed kind to say and to feel so, for I don't seem to myself to be so estimated by you. I am really worth but little except as a physician, and Harold here can outdo me in that line," he added, giving Harold a warmly affectionate look and smile.

"I must beg to differ as to that, Cousin Dick," returned Harold brightly. "I know of no physician to whom I would sooner trust the life of any ailing dear one than to yourself."

"Thanks, that is certainly a very strong endorsement you give me, sir," laughed Dick, coloring with pleasure.

"And I can give you the same," replied his half brother and partner, Dr. Johnson. "We seem to be a family of remarkably good physicians, if we do say so ourselves," he added with a merry laugh.

"I don't think you need. You may safely trust to other folks doing it," remarked Captain Raymond pleasantly.

"But don't expect any of us to get sick in order to give you fellows a chance to show your skill," observed Mr. Dinsmore gravely.

"Oh, no, uncle. We can find plenty of patients among the constant dwellers in this region. So, you may feel quite safe from our experimenting upon you—unless you get up an accident that will call for our aid," said Dick.

"I assure you I have no idea of doing that, even to help my nephews and grandson to plenty of employment to keep them out of mischief," laughed Mr. Dinsmore.

"And you needn't, grandpa, so far as I am concerned," said Harold with a humorous look and smile. "This is Gracie's and my honeymoon, you know, and we are entitled to a full holiday."

"So you are, and I shall do nothing to interfere with it," returned Mr. Dinsmore with assumed gravity but a twinkle of fun in his eye.

"Are Chester and Lu coming with the other party, uncle?" asked Maud.

"No, I understand that Chester has too much business calling for his attention, and that Lu, like the good, affectionate wife that she is, could not be persuaded to leave him. Eva remains at home for their sake and that of her baby."

And so the talk went on until all the courses of the grand dinner had been served and heartily partaken of.

Then all, old and young, gathered in the drawing room and spent a pleasant hour in friendly chat. After that, cordial goodnights were exchanged, accompanied with plans and promises in regard to future intentions, and one after another the relatives and guests departed for their own homes.

Little, feeble Ned had already been taken to his nest for the night, but the other children were now permitted a brief sojourn upon the front veranda, which was made delightful by the sweet scent of the orange blossoms upon the trees and the many lovely flowers adorning the moonlighted lawn, that light giving them also a charming view of the more distant landscape.

CHAPTER
FOURTEENTH

IT WAS A VERY bright, cheerful party that gathered about the Viamede breakfast table the next morning.

"Southern air seems to agree finely with my young patient thus far," remarked Dr. Harold, looking smilingly at Ned, who was partaking of the good fare provided with an appetite such as he had not shown before since the beginning of his illness.

"Yes, uncle, I'm hungry this morning, and everything tastes good," laughed Ned. "But Viamede victuals always were ever so nice."

"And home victuals poor and tasteless?" queried the lad's mother, feigning a look of grieved surprise.

"Oh, no, mamma. Home victuals are good— very good—when one is well, so as to have a good appetite," returned Ned reassuringly.

"Very true, son," said his father, "and you used to show full appreciation of them. So mamma need not feel hurt that you so greatly enjoy your present fare."

"And p'raps his good appetite will make the little chap strong enough for a row on the bayou a bit arter gittin' done his breakfast," said a rough voice, seemingly coming from an open doorway into the outer hall.

"Now, who are you, talking that way about me?" queried Ned, turning half way around in his chair in an effort to catch sight of the speaker.

"Who am I? Somebody that knows a thing or two 'bout boys an' what they can do, an' what they like. An' I guess you're not much different from any other fellows o' your age an' sect. Be ye now?"

"No, I guess not," laughed Ned. "I don't belong to any sect, though. But I suppose you mean sex. I'm of the male kind."

"Oh, you are. Then I s'pose you're brave enough to venture a row on the bayou without fear o' bein' drowned?"

"Yes, indeed, with all of these grown-up folks along to take care of me," laughed Ned. Then looking across the table at Mr. Lilburn, "Now that was just you talking, Cousin Ronald. Wasn't it?"

"Why, Neddie boy, do you think that is the kind of English I speak?" queried Mr. Lilburn in a hurt tone, as if he felt insulted by such a suspicion in regard to his knowledge and use of the English tongue.

"No, Cousin Ronald, I didn't mean any harm. But haven't you different kinds of voices for different times and occasions?" returned Ned.

"And weren't you kindly trying to make a bit of fun for me?"

"Ah, little chap, you seem to be very good at guessing," laughed Mr. Lilburn. "A bit of a Yankee, aren't you?"

"No, sir. I'm a whole one," cried Ned, echoing the laugh. "But, papa," turning to his father, "can we get a boat and have a row on the bayou?"

"Well, Ned, I suppose that might be possible," was the smiling rejoinder. "Suppose we take a vote on the question. All in favor of that fine proposition say 'aye'."

At that, there was a unanimous aye from the voice of each at the table.

Then Grandma Elsie said, "I think it would be enjoyable, but probably the cousins may be coming in to make their party calls before we get back."

"I think not, mamma, if we start early and do not go far," said Violet. "We can leave word with the servants that our absence will be short, so that anyone who comes will be encouraged to wait a bit."

"I should think they well might," smilingly added Mrs. Lilburn, "seeing what a delightful place they would have to wait in and plenty of interesting reading matter at hand."

"Yes, I think we really might venture it," said Dr. Harold, "especially as the little jaunt will probably be for the health of all taking part in it."

So it was decided upon, and the plan carried out shortly after leaving the table.

Everyone, especially the younger folk, seemed delighted with the idea and eager for the start. Ned was well wrapped up under the supervision of his mother and uncle and seated in a part of the boat where there could not be any danger for him of even a slight wetting.

All found it a delightful trip and returned refreshed and strengthened, the younger ones full of mirth and jollity.

It so happened that they were just in time to greet an arrival of cousins from Magnolia Hall and the Parsonage, presently followed by those from Torriswood. Cordial greetings were exchanged and an hour or two spent in pleasant interaction, in which plans were laid for excursions here and there through the lovely surrounding country and entertainments at one and another of their homes.

"Don't wait for the coming of the rest of your party of relatives," said Dr. Percival. "We will look forward to the pleasure of having you all again with that agreeable addition to the company."

"Thank you, Dick," returned Grandma Elsie with her own sweet smile. "We can hardly have more than would be agreeable of these lovely excursions or the delightful visits to the hospitable homes of our kith and kin in this region. And the oftener any or all of you visit us here at Viamede, the better."

"And please understand that we all echo in our hearts the sentiments just expressed by our dearly beloved mother," supplemented Violet in her sprightly way.

"Yes," laughed the captain. "I can vouch for the correctness of my wife's strong assertion."

"And I," added Harold, "join with my brother physician in recommending for the health, as well as present enjoyment of us all, the taking of an unlimited number of these delightful excursions by land and water."

"Now let's follow that good prescription," laughed Elsie Dinsmore, and the other young people received the suggestion with clapping of hands and words of most decided approval.

A merry, enjoyable fortnight followed before the expected increase in their numbers, during which Cousin Ronald often entertained them with exhibitions of his skill as a ventriloquist. It did not mystify and puzzle them as it had done when they first made his acquaintance, but, nevertheless, it was the exciting cause of much mirth and hilarity. Especially when there happened to be some neighbor present who was ignorant of the old gentleman's peculiar talent. It often made the call of such casual acquaintances all the more desirable and welcome. The relatives from Magnolia Hall, Torriswood, and the Parsonage were often visitors at Viamede, sitting with its family on the veranda in the afternoons and evenings, and quite frequently callers, more or less intimate, would be there with them. If Mr. Lilburn felt in the mood or was urged by one or more of the young folks of the family to try his skill, he would kindly do so.

Early one evening, when the gathering was larger than usual, Ned crept to Cousin Ronald's side and whispered in his ear an urgent request for a bit of the fun he alone could make. "Perhaps, sonny boy, if an idea comes to me," replied the old gentleman in the same low key. "Go back now to your mother and be quiet and easy for your health's sake."

Ned obeyed, and leaning on his mother's lap with her arm around him, listened eagerly for he hardly knew exactly what.

Presently a voice was heard, seemingly coming from a clump of bushes not far away, "Ladies and gentlemen, young folks, too, what good times you're having! While I'm but a poor fellow, wandering and homeless in a strange land with no roof to cover me, no bed to sleep in, and nothing to eat. Ah, woe's me! What can I do but lie down and die?"

"No, you needn't," called out Ned. "Go around to the kitchen and ask politely for something to eat, and you'll get it."

"I don't believe they'd give me a bite. I'm not a beggar, either, an' to take to that trade wad be far worse than a-dyin' as an honest, upright, an' self-supporting man."

"Why, who is it, and what does he want?" queried one of Viamede's visitors in tones of surprise and disgust.

"Let's go down and see. Give him some money, if he'll take it, to buy himself some supper and to pay for a night's lodging," said another guest, jumping up and moving quickly toward the veranda steps.

"Tell him we'll give him something to eat—send it out there to him, if he wishes," said Grandma Elsie, speaking very soberly, though she felt pretty certain they would find no one there.

The lads hurried down to the bushes that seemed to hide the stranger, and Ned clapped his hands in ecstasy over the idea that they had been so easily and completely duped.

"They'll be greatly surprised and disappointed," said Elsie Dinsmore. "It's almost too bad, for they seem very kindhearted and ready to help one in obvious distress."

The other young folks were laughing in an amused way.

"And it was just you, Cousin Ronald. Wasn't it?" asked Elsie Raymond.

"Why, what a strange idea!" exclaimed the old gentleman. "I haven't been down there on the lawn for hours."

"But maybe your voice has," laughed Elsie. "Oh, here they come to tell us about it," exclaimed Alie Leland, as the lads were seen hurrying back in a very excited way.

"There's nobody there!" cried one. "We searched all about and couldn't find a soul."

"No, indeed, we couldn't, and it's very, very mysterious, I think," added the other.

"Looks as if he'd run off before you got there," said Ned.

"He couldn't. There wasn't time," panted the foremost lad as they came slowly up the steps of the veranda.

"Well, then it's his own fault if he misses getting something to eat," said Ned, trying hard to keep from laughing.

"Strange how blind some folks are," remarked the strange voice, seeming now close to the veranda and followed by a profound sigh.

"Why, there he is again and nearer than before!" cried one of the lads who had been trying to find him, and both peered eagerly over the railing. But to their evdent astonishment, they could see no one.

"Dear me, where in the world is he?" exclaimed again the boy who had first spoken. "His voice sounded even nearer than before, and yet he's nowhere to be seen."

"Oh, let's look yonder under the veranda," suggested the other. "Perhaps he may have crept in there."

"Oh, yes, if Mrs. Travilla is willing," returned his companion.

"I have no objection," she said pleasantly, and they proceeded to look but soon announced that there was no one to be found there.

"And it certainly isn't worth your while to take such trouble to find so good for naught a scamp," returned Mr. Lilburn in his natural voice. "I wadna try it anymore, lads."

"Ha, ha, ha. I knew you couldn't find me!" laughed the invisible speaker, the voice this time apparently coming from the roof of the veranda.

"Well," cried Ned, "how in the world did he get up there? What a famous climber he must be to scamper up there so quickly!"

At that, the mystified boys hurried down the veranda steps again and some little distance down the path leading across the grounds from the front of the dwelling, from which they could turn and look up at the veranda's roof.

"Why, there's nothing and nobody there!" they exclaimed breathlessly as they hurried back again to the veranda.

"It certainly is a most mysterious thing," panted one. "How a fellow could be so close by and then disappear so suddenly and completely, I can't imagine."

"Well, well, lads, such a slippery ne'er-do-well isna worth worrying about," said Mr. Lilburn. "We needna trouble oursel's if he goes hungry."

"But I should be sorry indeed to have any of my guests do that," said Grandma Elsie as just at that moments servants appeared carrying silver salvers laden with fruit and cakes.

That seemed a welcome interruption to even the sorely puzzled stranger boys, and when that feasting was over, the captain called for music. His wife, going to the piano, played *Yankee Doodle* with variation, the *Star-spangled Banner*, in the singing of which all joined heartily. Just as the last strain died away, the strange voice was heard again from the far end of the veranda.

"That's a grand old song. Just the kind for every American to sing, whether he's rich or poor. It doesn't matter."

"Oh, there he is again!" cried the stranger lads, springing to their feet and looking eagerly in the direction of the sounds.

"But just as invisible as ever," gasped one. "How on earth does he manage to disappear so quickly?"

At that there was a half-suppressed ripple of laughter among the young folks of the house, while Mr. Lilburn said in his own natural tones, "Tut, tut, young fellows. I'd pay no attention to him. He isn't worth minding."

"No, indeed," said Dr. Harold. "He isn't and wouldn't attempt to harm any one of us, even if he wanted to, as we are so many and he but one."

"No," said the voice, "I'm not worth minding and not at all dangerous, for I wouldn't hurt anybody if I wanted to and wouldn't dare do it if I had such a wicked inclination."

"Well, sir, it's very, very strange how you can be so plainly heard and not seen at all," remarked one of the puzzled young fellows. Then pulling out his watch, "Well, it's high time for me to go home now."

"For me, too," said his companion, and bidding goodnight to their hostess and the company, they went away together.

"Good! They didn't find out anything about Cousin Ronald," chuckled Ned when they were beyond hearing.

Then began plans for the next day's outing, and conjectures as to when they might look for the expected addition to this Viamede party from their more northern homes. That was brought about in a few days and added great pleasure to their picnics, excursions, and family gatherings at Torriswood, Magnolia Hall, the Parsonage, and Viamede itself.

CHAPTER
FIFTEENTH

To Lucilla it seemed very hard to part for months after the wedding from her darling sister Gracie and from Elsie and Ned also, to say nothing of Harold and his lovely mother. For the fortnight or more that elapsed before the other company left, she clung very closely to her father and Max, not neglecting Violet either. But when they also were gone, she gave herself more unreservedly to Eva and baby Mary, enjoying them keenly through the day while business claimed Chester's attention and then to him in the evenings and early mornings until he must hie away to his office in Uniontown.

During the time that elapsed between the departure of the first and second party of relatives and friends to the South, there was an almost daily exchange of visits with the Oaks and Fairview families and those at Ion also, and it was a joy to know that they—the Ion people—were not to flit with the others. Roseland and Beechwood friends had also planned to remain at home through the winter, and it was particularly welcome to Lucilla that Drs. Arthur Conly and Herbert Travilla were evidently intending to do likewise, except as they traveled about the adjacent country in the practice of their profession. The Ion family—Edward Travilla, his wife, and children—having visited Viamede only the year before, were expecting to spend their winter at their own home, and Zoe, with kindhearted concern for Evelyn and Lucilla, made frequent little visits to Sunnyside, which she urgently invited them to return. They did so when there were no more important calls upon their time and the weather was suitable for little Mary to be taken out—for to both mother and aunt she seemed too dear and precious to be left behind.

Then there was the pleasant task of the daily correspondence with their nearest and dearest of absent relatives and friends—Eva with her husband, father-in-law, and Violet and Lucilla with her father, brother, and sister. How delightful it was to get their letters. How eagerly they both watched for the coming of the daily mail.

Lucilla sadly missed her morning strolls with her father about the grounds, yet not so much as she might have done at another season of the year. For it was often too cold and stormy for such rambles even had he been there. She would console herself with writing to him what she might have said with her tongue had he been there to listen to her loving, daughterly confidences and expressions of affection. And she could seek his wise counsels and receive them in his answering epistle. So she strove to be patient and content, rejoicing in the glad hope that the separation was to be for but a few short months.

"And," she would say to herself, "how much better off I am than poor, dear Eva, my husband coming home every night, while hers is to be gone for weeks or months."

Evelyn sorely missed her absent husband, but the darling baby daughter was a great joy and comfort to her.

So passed January, February, and March, and with the coming in of April, Eva and Lucilla rejoiced in the thought that in a few weeks the dear ones now at Viamede would be returning to their more northern homes. Pleased, too, were the Ion folks and the kith and kin, or those left in charge, at the Oaks, Fairview, Beechwood, Roselands, the Laurels, and Riverside.

Dr. Arthur Conley and his Marian, strongly attached to each other and almost idolizing their baby boy, were an ideally happy pair, and Roselands had grown even more lovely that it was in earlier days. As they were about to leave the breakfast table one fair April morning, a ring from the telephone bell summoned the doctor to make a prompt call at Sunnyside.

He replied that he would be there as soon as possible, which would be in a few minutes, as his gig was already at the door. Turning about, he found his wife close at his side.

"I must set off at once for Sunnyside," he said. "Lucilla is needing a doctor. Will you go along?"

"Yes, indeed. She has been such a kind friend to me that I love her as if she were my own sister. We can safely trust our darling, little Ronald for an hour or two to the care of his nurse."

"With perfect safety. She is his devoted servant," laughed the doctor.

So the two set off at once on their errand of mercy and loving kindness.

They found Chester at home, Dr. Herbert Travilla already there, Lucilla in bed, suffering but patient, Zoe from Ion and Ella from Beechwood already there to do what they could for her, and Eva, passing in and out, anxious to do all in her power, yet not willing to neglect baby Mary.

An hour or two later, a baby boy was gently laid down by Lucilla's side.

"Your son, dearest," Chester said in rapturous tones, "the little Levis Raymond we have been hoping for."

"Oh, how glad I am!" she cried. "My father's first grandson, bearing his name. Baby dear, you shall be your mother's 'Ray of Sunshine.' Oh, how I want to show you to my father, your own grandfather."

"There, love," Chester said, giving her a kiss of ardent affection, "that will do. Don't talk any more now, lest you wear yourself out."

"That is good advice, Cousin Lu, and I hope you will follow it," said Dr. Conly. "You must take care of yourself now for the sake of your husband and son."

"I will," she answered, "but, oh, Chester, send word to father and the others as soon as you can."

"Dearest," he said with a happy laugh, "I have already done so. Before leaving us, he charged me not to delay a moment to let him know if you were taken ill and to send word promptly. I have obeyed."

"And he will soon be here to see this, his first grandson! I am so glad I could give him one," she exclaimed in tones of delight.

"As I am," responded Chester. "But, love, don't talk any more just now, but try for a nap such as the tiny newcomer seems to be taking."

"I will, if only to please and satisfy you, my dear husband," she returned with a happy little laugh, and almost instantly she passed into the land of dreams, while Chester softly withdrew from the room, leaving her in the charge of a skillful, trustworthy nurse.

He found Eva with her baby and Marian, the other ladies, and the doctors on the front veranda.

"You are looking very happy, Chester," laughed Dr. Herbert, "almost as if you had fallen into a fortune since I came here this morning."

"Pretty much as I feel," returned Chester, his countenance telling more of joy and thankfulness than his tongue. "Lu has fallen into a comfortable sleep," he went on. "The little newcomer seems to be as welcome to her as to me."

"And I think my wife and I can fully appreciate your joy over him," said Dr. Conly, exchanging an affectionate, smiling glance with his Marian.

"The telephone has already carried the news to all our relatives in this neighborhood and brought pleased and congratulatory replies," said Herbert. "You phoned her father. Did you not, Chester?"

"Yes," replied Chester, "and there, no doubt, comes his response," he added, as the ringing of his telephone was heard at that moment. "So now we may learn how he feels." He hastened to the instrument, the others following, all eager to learn what the message from the absent loved ones might be.

The captain's message was one of thankfulness and ardent parental love for his dear daughter, who, he hoped, would soon be well and strong. He was glad to have a grandson and appreciated the naming of the child for him.

"A most kind, affectionate message," remarked Chester with a sigh of satisfaction as he turned from the instrument to Eva and the others. "Lu will be pleased when I tell her what her father says. How she does love and cling to him! I am glad, indeed, that we may hope to see him and all the party here again in a few weeks."

"So am I," said Dr. Conley. "In the meantime, we will do our best to bring Lu safely back to her usual robust health and strength."

"And to have her son in a like flourishing condition," added Dr. Herbert with genial look and smile directed to the father of the little lad.

CHAPTER
SIXTEENTH

CAPTAIN RAYMOND was sitting alone in the library at Viamede, busily engaged in examining and answering letters received by that morning's mail when the telephone brought him Chester's message in regard to Lucilla—her illness and the birth of their little son. It was news of deepest interest and importance to the loving, anxious father. He answered at once and then went out into the grounds to seek his wife, who, with Elsie and Ned, had remained at home while the rest of their party and neighbor friends had gone off on various excursions by land or water.

Ned was not strong enough to be continually on the go, and his parents and sister had elected to stay at home with him on this occasion. Violet was now sitting under the orange tree with a child on each side, who were listening with keen interest to a story that she was reading to them. She paused at the sound of her husband's footsteps and looking up into his face, laughingly exclaimed, "Why, how happy you look, my dear! Have you good news?"

"Yes, love," he replied. "We have a grandson, and mother and child seem to be doing well."

"Oh, papa, a grandson! Why, whose baby is it? Another one for Eva?" queried Elsie in great excitement at the news.

"No, it is your sister Lu who is the mother this time, and Chester is his father."

"Oh, a dear little boy! I wish we were there to see him," cried Ned.

"I hope to take you there in a few weeks," returned his father with a pleased smile. "We won't delay much longer, for I should really like a sight of the little fellow myself."

"As I certainly should," said Violet. "Dear Lu! I have no doubt she is very happy over it. And they have named him for you. Haven't they, Levis?"

"Yes, my dear wife, for me, his only living grandsire," returned the captain, tone and accompanying smile both showing the pleasure he felt in being thus affectionately remembered by both parents of the little one.

"Yes, so you are, and I should have been exceedingly surprised had they given the child any other name. For Lu loves you with all her heart, and Chester seems to feel quite as if you were his own father."

"I believe that is so," returned the captain, his tone and countenance expressing satisfaction. "I am fortunate as concerns my sons-in-law, except in the mixture of the relationships in the gaining of the last, and that has seemed to work well enough thus far, even so."

"I think it does, and it has ceased to trouble me," said Violet. "But this news makes me feel like hurrying home to Woodburn, and I am sure will have that effect upon Gracie when she hears it."

"I dare say," assented the captain, "and I think we need not linger here at Viamede longer than another fortnight."

❧ ❧ ❧ ❧ ❧

"I am so glad," cried Gracie when she heard the news. "Lu wanted to give you your first grandson, and now she has got her wish."

"I fully appreciate the affection that prompted the wish and am glad, especially for her sake, that it was granted," returned the captain with a look that said even more than words.

"As I am," said Harold, "especially as I know that it was Chester's wish as much as hers."

The Torriswood folk had come in with the Travillas, and now they expressed their apparent gratification at the news.

"A little nephew for us," exclaimed Maud. "And I am glad for Chester as well as Lu, as it seems he wanted it, but I'm glad our baby is a girl that we could name for dear Cousin Elsie," giving a warmly loving look to Grandma Elsie as she spoke.

"As I am," said her husband, adding, "and I only hope that a close resemblance in both looks and character may accompany the name."

"As I do in regard to my little darling," said Sydney and Dr. Johnson, speaking simultaneously. Then they laughed, and Sydney added, "I shall write to the happy parents, offering my warm congratulations."

"And I shall do likewise," said Maud, "telling them I am glad I am now aunt to the wonderful little chap."

"And I shall write to Lu that she may consider me both his cousin and his grandma," laughed Violet brightly.

"Oh, mamma," exclaimed her daughter Elsie, "you know I don't like to have you called a grandma. It sounds as if you were old, and you are not at all old."

"Well, dear child, you needn't mind. It won't make me a day older," laughed Violet.

"Nor me, although it would seem to make me a great-grandmother again," added Grandma Elsie pleasantly.

"While no one would suspect you from your looks of being even a grandmother," remarked the captain gallantly.

"No," said Dr. Percival. "I have seen many much younger women who looked a great deal older than you, Cousin Elsie."

"Oh, Dick, Dick, Cousin Dick, don't you turn flatterer," she laughed, though looking not at all displeased. "Though I am not very sorry to hear such flattering remarks, as they are evidently pleasing to my children."

"Indeed they are," said Violet, "and are all the more so because we see that they are all perfectly truthful."

"Well, it is high time that we busy doctors and proposed letter writers were going home," said Dr. Percival, rising to take leave. "Yes," said Maud, following his example, "especially as Elsie P. and Elsie J. must be wanting their mothers by this time."

"So we are off for Torriswood," said Sydney. "Good-bye, dear friends and relatives, till next time. We hope to have this call returned this evening or tomorrow morning," and with that, the four took their departure.

"And I must write at once to dear Lu a letter of warm congratulations," said Gracie, following her father into the library and being herself followed by Harold, who intended to do likewise.

They were all letters which, when received by Lucilla, seemed to her very sweet and refreshing, her father's even more so than either of the other two. But before they reached her, she and Chester had had several messages from him by telegram and telephone. And all these were shared with Evelyn—Lucilla's constant, loved companion and dear sister. Most of them also by the nearby friends and relatives, whose love and sympathy were shown by almost daily calls and hours of pleasant interaction.

No one showed more sympathy and kindness to Lu than Zoe, Mrs. Edward Travilla.

"I am glad for you, Lu, that your baby is a boy, since that is what you wanted," she remarked to Lucilla one day. "But for my part, if I have another child, I hope it may be a girl, so that I can name her for mamma. She is and has always been such a dear, kind mother to me."

"Yes, she is certainly one of the dearest and sweetest of women," responded Lucilla heartily. "But there are so many Elsies that it really seems a little confusing. I believe I should rather like to have one myself if that were not the case," she added laughingly, "for I do dearly love Grandma Elsie, as I have been used to calling her. My, what a mixed-up set we are becoming! For, as you know, she is now mother to my sister Gracie."

"Who, to my delight, is my sister now, since she is the wife of my husband's brother," returned Zoe exultingly.

"And mine, since I am the wife of her brother," laughed Evelyn. "Oh, we are a mixed-up set, but perhaps none the less happy and well off for that mixing up of relations."

"No, I think not," said Zoe.

"And I am quite sure of it," said Lucilla. "And as my husband is a distant relative of yours, Zoe, you and I can claim kin. Can't we?"

"Yes, and we will. We will call ourselves cousins from this time forward."

"And as my Aunt Elsie, Grandma Elsie's oldest daughter, is sister to your husband, can't you and I claim kin, Zoe?" asked Evelyn.

"Certainly," promptly replied Zoe. "We will consider ourselves cousins."

"So we will. It is a very comfortable way to settle matters," laughed Evelyn. "We have been calling you Aunt Zoe, but you are too young for that, and we have been growing up to you in age."

"So you have. Well, how soon do you expect our kith and kin to come from Viamede to their more northern homes?"

"Father says in two or three weeks," replied Lucilla, "and I hope I shall be allowed to sit up by that time. Oh, you don't know how I long to show him my little Ray of Sunshine!" she added, gently patting the sleeping babe by her side. "Oh, both Chester and I want very much to have him resemble his grandfather, my dear father, in looks, character, and everything."

"As I hope and believe he will," said Zoe in tones of sympathy and encouragement.

※※※※※※※※

CHAPTER
SEVENTEENTH

AT VIAMEDE, Chester's daily message by telephone or telegraph was eagerly awaited and greatly rejoiced over, as it reported steady improvement in Lucilla's health—constantly gaining in strength—and the new baby also in a most flourishing condition. All wanted to see him, but no one more than Gracie, who felt that the child of her beloved sister must and would be very near and dear to her, while to the others he was fully as near and dear as darling baby Mary.

They would have returned home immediately but for the fact that Dr. Harold and his brother physicians considered it safer for both Gracie and Ned to remain in the warmer climate until some day late in May.

The older Mr. and Mrs. Dinsmore and the Oaks and Fairview families went home somewhat earlier, traveling by rail, but Mr. and Mrs. Lilburn accepted an invitation to return in the *Dolphin*, as did Grandma Elsie. Of course, Gracie and Harold were to be passengers in her, making with Violet, her two children, and the captain himself quite a party—actually much the same party that had come in her.

During these weeks of waiting, they continued their pleasant little excursions by land and water and their sociable evening parties on the veranda or out under the trees, which were generally enlivened by exhibitions of Cousin Ronald's ventriloquial skill or made interesting by a bit of history or some sort of story told by Captain Raymond or Grandma Elsie.

On Sunday mornings, they all attended church and heard a sermon by their pastor, the Reverend Cyril Keith, and in the afternoon the servants and other persons of the neighborhood were invited to assemble on the lawn when the captain would give them a brief and plain discourse about the dear Lord Jesus and His dying love, making the way of salvation very clear and plain. They would have prayer, too, and the singing of gospel hymns.

In the evening, the captain would catechize his own children, and there would be religious conversation and the singing of hymns. They were sweet, peaceful, improving Sabbaths, enjoyable at the time and pleasant to look back upon.

It was on a lovely morning in the latter part of May that they left beautiful Viamede and sailed away for their more northern homes, going with mingled feelings of joy and sorrow, for how could they leave Viamede or part with the dear relatives in that region without regret? Or how could they fail to rejoice in the prospect of soon seeing the sweet homes for which they were now bound and the tenderly loved ones there?

Harold was very happy in the consciousness of being able to take both Gracie and Ned back to their homes in almost perfect health, and very careful was he to watch against any exposure for them to wind or weather that might result in the renewal of any of their ailments. When the weather was bright, clear, and not too cold, he encouraged them to be on the deck in the bracing air, but in cloudy or damp weather, he insisted on their remaining below in salon or stateroom.

At such times Grandma Elsie, Cousin Ronald, or the captain would be called upon to provide entertainment, and one or another was sure to comply with the request.

"Papa," said Elsie Raymond on one of those occasions, "I should like it very much if you would give us a little history of Texas."

"If I should attempt to give you all its history, it would be a long story," he said with a smile, "but I shall give a brief outline and try to make it interesting. I want you to have some knowledge of the early history of each of our states.

"A colony of Frenchmen were the first whites who settled in Texas. They were lead by la Salle. He meant to found a colony near the mouth of the Mississippi, but by mistake he entered Matagorda Bay, went five or six miles up the Lavaca, and there built Fort St. Louis. That was about the year 1686. In the spring of the next year, he was murdered by his men. They had been quarrelling and killing each other, and when the Indians heard of the death of la Salle, they attacked the fort and killed all the men left but four, whom they carried into captivity. Some two years later, a Spanish expedition sailed into Matagorda Bay, intending to drive away the French, but they found they were gone and the fort destroyed. A few years afterward, several settlements were made in that state—what is now Texas—by the Spaniards, but soon they abandoned them because of Indian hostilities.

"It seems that both the Spaniards and the French considered the province their own, though it did not really belong to either of them, for the Indians were the rightful owners. In 1712, Louis XIV of France granted it to Crozat, the same man to whom he had granted Louisiana. That so alarmed the Spaniards in Mexico that they promptly made numerous settlements in Texas, thinking in that way to secure the province for themselves. The French tried to expel them, but they did not succeed.

"Some years later four hundred families were sent by the Spanish government from the Canary Isles to Texas and were joined there by others from Mexico. These families founded the city of San Antonio.

"For some time, the Indians of Texas and Louisiana were very troublesome, but in 1732, the Spaniards defeated them in a great battle and so quieted them for some years.

"You know our Revolutionary War began in 1775. Spain declared war against England in 1779 and carried on active hostilities against the British on the Mississippi River. Then a prosperous trade was carried on between the Spanish settlement of Natchez in Mississippi and the interior of Texas. This became the means of making that province known to the Americans.

"After the Untied States came into possession of Louisiana, a treaty between them and Spain fixed the Sabine River as the eastern boundary of Texas upon the Gulf. West of that river was a tract called the Neutral Ground, which was then occupied by bands of outlaws and desperate men, who lived by robbery and plunder. The Spanish authorities had tried to expel them, but they could not. Our government sent a force against them and drove them away, but they came back and went on with their robberies.

"About that time, a civil war was raging in Mexico, and that favored the plans of a man who wanted to conquer Texas to the Rio Grande and establish a republican government. There was a good deal of fighting and much slaughter of both Americans and Spaniards, the latter being victors in the end, but I shall not go into particulars at this time but leave you young people to read the whole sad story when you are older. For years, there was fighting, wounding, killing, the Mexicans murdering many Americans in cold blood after they had surrendered as prisoners of war. But at last, the independence of Texas was secured. And after a little while, she asked to be annexed to the United States, a request which was finally granted. By a joint resolution of Congress, she was annexed to the Union on February 28, 1845."

"She seceded at the time of the Civil War. Did she not, papa?" asked Gracie.

"Yes," he replied, "but she was readmitted into the Union in March of 1870."

"Texas is a very big state. Isn't it, papa?" asked little Elsie.

"Yes, the largest of all our states," he replied, "and it has every variety of surface—plain, mountain, hill, and desert. Its coast is lined with a chain of low islands, forming a series of bays, lagoons, and sounds. There are a number of rivers, several of them very long—eighteen hundred miles is the length of the Rio Grande, which is the largest of them. It forms the southwestern boundary. There is a salt lake near it, from which large quantities of salt are taken every year."

"The climate is warm, there. Is it not, papa?" asked Gracie.

"Yes," he said, "it claims to be called the Italy of America. It has a delightful, unwavering summer sea breeze, and the nights are always cool enough to make a blanket acceptable, even when the day has been oppressively hot. But now that surely is enough of that one state for today."

"Yes, papa, and many thanks to you for giving us so interesting an account," said Gracie. Elsie and Ned added their thanks. Then Elsie took up a book, and Ned went to his berth for a nap.

CHAPTER
EIGHTEENTH

GRANDMA ELSIE, VIOLET, and Gracie were all sewing on some delicate pink silk material, trimming it with bows of ribbon of the same color and duchess lace. Young Elsie presently drew near and asked what they were making.

"Guess," laughed her mother. "What does it look like?"

"As if it might be going to be a baby afghan," ventured the little girl. "Oh, is it one for Lu's new baby?"

"It is," returned her mother. "You must be a bit of a Yankee to guess so well."

"I believe I am, as papa says he is one," replied Elsie. "I hope it will be as pretty as the one you made for baby Mary's carriage. Oh, are you going to give little Ray a carriage, too?"

"Yes, indeed. We must do all for him that we did for his little cousin."

"But you used different colors. That way, they will always know which is which. Isn't that why you do it that way, mamma?"

"Yes, for that reason and because of the different complexions of the two children. Mary is fair with golden hair and blue eyes, while Ray has his mother's dark eyes and hair."

"Oh, yes, and I think it's nice that they differ in that way and really suppose one is just as pretty as the other. Anyhow, I expect to think so, because I'm aunt to both of them."

"That's right," laughed her mother. "Be as impartial as you can."

"Mary we know to be a dear little thing, whom no one with any heart could help loving," said Grandma Elsie, "and I am pretty certain we will find Ray equally lovable."

"And isn't he a relation to you, grandma?" asked Elsie.

"Yes, through his father, who is a Dinsmore—a cousin of mine. Lucilla's married name is the same as was my maiden name."

"And Lu is my sister, and that makes me aunt to the dear little fellow, just as I am to Max's little daughter. I think it's nice to be aunt to such dear babies."

From that time on, Elsie watched with great interest the work of getting the little coach quite ready for its intended baby owner, which was entirely completed before the *Dolphin* reached the dock at Uniontown. In the mean-time, great preparations for the coming of her passengers had been going on at Woodburn, Ion, the Laurels, Riverside, Fairview, Roselands, Sunnyside, and Beechwood. Nearly all of the relatives from those places met them on the landing ready to convey them to their homes, or wherever they might want to go. But that was to Woodburn for all, the captain told them, great preparations having been made there, by his orders sent on some days previously, for a great welcoming feast.

The Woodburn and Sunnyside carriages were in waiting and were entered as soon as the glad greetings had been exchanged, and all went on their way rejoicing.

Lucilla, now quite able to be up and about, was in the library with her babe sleeping in a crib by her side. She would stay there, she told Eva, who, with her baby, sat there with her. She would want her father to come to her there and see her and Ray alone before she could meet the others. "I want a private interview first, if only for five minutes," she said. "Then I shall be ready and glad to see the others."

"I shall see that it is as you wish, dear sister," said Evelyn, and she kept her word. The captain met her and baby Mary as he stepped upon the veranda. He gave a warm embrace to each and sent a hurried glance around, evidently in search of his daughter, Lucilla.

"Lu wants to see you alone first, father, to show you her baby boy—your first grandson—with no one else to look on," Evelyn said with a smile. "She is in the library waiting for you."

"Ah, yes," he said. He hastened there while the others were all still engaged in the exchange of greetings to the returning travelers.

As he entered, Lucilla started to her feet with a glad cry of, "Oh, father, father, my own dear father!"

He caught her in his arms and held her fast, caressing her with exceeding tenderness.

"My darling, my own dear, dear child. God be praised that I come home to find you here restored to usual health and strength."

"And you, father? You are well?" she asked, looking lovingly into his eyes.

"Quite well, daughter mine," he answered with another tender caress, "and if I were not, the sight of this dear child of mine would be almost enough to make me so."

"And the sight of your new grandchild, your first grandson, might help the cure. Might it not?" she answered with a proud, joyful glance directed at the tiny sleeper in the crib.

"Ah, what a darling!" her father said, releasing her and leaning over the crib. "His grandfather's heart has wide room in it for him. He is a beautiful babe in his grandsire's eyes and a dear one to his grandfather's heart. I feel very rich with two lovely grandchildren."

"May I come in?" asked Violet's voice at the door to the library.

"Oh, yes, indeed, Mamma Vi," answered Lucilla in joyous tones. "How glad I am to have you at home again," she added as they exchanged a hearty embrace. "Now, please come and look at my baby boy, my little Ray of Sunshine from Sunnyside," she added with a gleeful laugh.

Violet's expressed admiration was quite equal to the mother's wishes. "Oh, he is a lovely little fellow!" she exclaimed, leaning over the crib as his grandfather had done. "It's so fortunate that he is a boy. Now we have both a granddaughter and a grandson."

Just then Gracie's voice at the door asked, "May I come in?"

"Indeed you may!" cried Lucilla, running to meet her with delighted look and outstretched arms. "Oh, Gracie dear, how I have been longing for you—to see your dear face and to show you my new treasure, my son and your nephew. Come and look at him."

The words were accompanied by an ardent embrace each to the other. Then Lucilla drew Gracie to the side of the crib, the captain and Violet making room for her there. Bending over it, she exclaimed, "Oh, Lu, what a darling, beautiful little fellow! As pretty, as lovely, and as sweet looking as Max and Eva's little Mary, whom we all love so dearly."

Just then, other voices were heard at the door, asking permission to enter. They were familiar voices—those of Dr. Harold, Elsie, and Ned—and it being granted, the children rushed in, the doctor following with the baby carriage that had been trimmed on board the *Dolphin*.

"A gift for that young gentleman from his loving grandsire and grandma, Mrs. Dinsmore," he announced with a graceful bow to Lucilla.

"Oh," she cried, clapping her hands in delight, "what a beauty! Thank you, father dear, and you, too, Mamma Vi, and Gracie. For the beautiful work is yours, I know. Oh, how good and kind you all are to me and my baby boy!" She was fussing over the pretty little vehicle and its adornment as she spoke. "What lovely lace and ribbons, the colors exactly such as will show off to the best advantage my baby boy's complexion, hair, and eyes. It is a delightful surprise, for I was not expecting anything of the kind."

"I am very glad it pleases you, my daughter," her father said with his own kind smile, laying a hand affectionately upon her shoulder.

"As I am," said Violet, "and I want you to know that mamma helped largely with the work of trimming this little coach. Your baby boy is related to her, she says."

"Yes, and I am glad to know it," smiled Lucilla. "I am very glad that my marriage gives me some small claim to relationship to her. No one could have a right to claim it to a better, lovelier, or dearer person."

"That is quite true, daughter," the captain said with emotion.

At that moment, Chester came in with a pleased and cordial welcome to the returned travelers, and presently all went out together to join the others—returned travelers, relatives, and welcome guests.

To Grandma Elsie, Lucilla gave the warmest of greetings and thanks for her share in trimming the lovely little coach for her baby boy.

"You are very welcome, my dear. It was a labor of love," was the gentle-spoken, smiling response from Grandma Elsie.

There were hearty greetings, loving caresses, merry jests, and happy laughter. No one was weary, for voyaging in Captain Raymond's well-conditioned, well-furnished yacht was no strain upon the physical nature. His late passengers were, therefore, in prime condition, as were the other guests, coming from their own homes and not weary and worn with toil beyond their strength.

But soon came the call to the hospitable board laden with all the luxuries of the land and season, to which they brought good, healthful appetites and where were enjoyed also to the full the pleasures of social interaction between those nearly related and of similar views and temperaments. And that last went on after they had left the table for parlors and porches.

At length, the guests bid adieu until all had departed except the Sunnyside folk, who still sat on the veranda with the immediate Woodburn family. The babies were both awake now, each resting on their mother's laps or in her arms.

"I feel very rich with two such grandchildren," observed the captain, glancing with a happy smile from one to the other.

"As we do," laughed Chester, "though they are not our grandchildren. Don't we, Lu and Eva?"

Both ladies replied in the affirmative, each looking down with intense, joyful affection upon her little one.

"I should think you might, because they are both so pretty, sweet, and good," remarked their young Aunt Elsie.

"Of course, they are, and I'm glad to be their uncle," said Ned.

"As I am to be yours," said Dr. Harold, drawing him to a seat upon his knee. "Are you glad to be at home again?"

"Yes, sir, and glad that you are to live here in our house now, instead of taking Gracie away from us to some other place."

"I should be sorry, indeed, to take her away from you and the rest of the family here, and I don't think I shall ever carry her off very far from you and the others who love her so dearly," replied Harold. "But you wouldn't mind my going, if I left her behind with you. Would you?"

"Why of course I should, uncle. I might get sick again and perhaps die if I hadn't you to cure me."

"Oh, that needn't bother you while you have your other relatives—my brother Herbert and Dr. Arthur Conly. Either of them would be as likely to succeed in curing you as I."

"By the blessing of God upon their efforts," said the captain. "But without that no one could succeed at all."

"Most true, sir, and I did not mean to ignore that undeniable and important fact," said Dr. Harold. "I never use a remedy without craving His blessing upon it, and I desire to give Him all the glory and the praise."

"Yes, we know you do, brother dear," said Violet, "and that is why we are so ready to trust our dear ones to your care when they are ill."

"Please understand that I was not doubting that or your knowledge or skill," added Captain Raymond with a most cordial look and tone.

Just then a servant was seen coming up the driveway with two little monkeys in his arms.

"Oh," cried the children in delighted chorus, "there are our tee-tees. Ajax has brought them from Ion." They ran to meet him, holding out their arms to their pets.

"Yaas, I'se brung um, an' I reckon dey's glad to come," returned Ajax, loosening his hold. The little fellows sprang from his arms to those of their young master and mistress, who at once carried them up onto the veranda and exhibited them with great pride and pleasure, while the captain stepped down to the side of Ajax and rewarded him liberally for the service done and thanking him, too. He bid him carry warm thanks to those who had cared for the little animals and returned them in prime condition.

"We are so glad to get them back, the dear, funny, little fellows," remarked Elsie to Lucilla and Evelyn. "They will make fun for our little nephew and niece when they are old enough to understand and enjoy it."

"Thank you, Elsie dear," returned Eva with her own sweet smile.

"You are very kind, Elsie, to begin so soon to think of amusement for our babies," laughed

Lucilla, "and I hope you and Ned may be able to keep your monkeys alive and well till they are old enough to enjoy them."

"Yes, indeed, I hope so," responded Elsie. "I want both Mary and Ray to have lots of fun when they are old enough for it."

"Yes," said Dr. Harold, "I am always in favor of timely, innocent fun as a great promoter of good health."

"Yes," said Lucilla, "'laugh and grow fat' is an old adage, and we'll try to have our babies do it. Won't we, Eva?"

"I certainly intend to do all I can to make my darling bit lassie both healthy and happy," returned Evelyn, looking down with a tender, loving smile at the little one on her knee. "But fun and frolic need not fill up all the time. There is a quiet kind of happiness that would be better as a steady diet, I think, than constant frolic and fun. I hope she will be a contented little body, for there is much truth and wisdom in that other old adage, 'Contentment is better than wealth.'"

Both Violet and the captain expressed warm approval of her sentiments, as did Lucilla, Chester, and Dr. Harold also.

"But I'd like to have some fun now with our tee-tees," said Ned, patting his as he held it in his arms. "I wish we had Max or Cousin Ronald here to make them talk."

"I'd wish so, too, if it would do any good," said Elsie.

"No," laughed Lucilla, "it wouldn't, and I am reminded of the old saying, 'If wishes were horses, then beggars might ride.'"

"As you two are so glad to get your tee-tees back again, don't you feel sorry for Lily and Laurie that they had to part with them?" asked Violet quietly.

"Yes, mamma," replied Ned, "I do. But they have had them a good while."

"I'm sorry for them," Elsie said in a regretful tone. "I wish we could buy them tee-tees or something else that they'd like just as well."

"Perhaps we can," said their father. "We will think about it."

"Oh, papa, I'm glad to hear you say that," she said in joyous tones. "I do feel sorry for them."

"And so do I," said Ned. "I am sorry enough to give all the pocket money I have now to buy them something nice."

※ ※ ※ ※ ※ ※ ※ ※

CHAPTER
NINETEENTH

AT ION WAS NOW gathered as pleasant a family party as that now in session at Woodburn. Grandma Elsie was there with her father and his wife, her son Edward with Zoe, his wife, and their two children—the twins Laurie and Lily, Ion being their home. Herbert and Walter were also present. All the Fairview folk were there as well, for Mrs. Elsie Leland wanted a chat on family affairs and relatives with her mother, whom, until today, she had not seen for several weeks. This sort of chat they could not well take in the larger company of relatives and friends whose society they had just been enjoying at Woodburn. Mr. Leland and his children had naturally accompanied the wife and mother, knowing that they were always welcome guests at Ion.

They seemed to be enjoying themselves—the older ones in a quiet, cheerful way and the younger ones gathered in a separate group at the farther end of the veranda with a good deal of fun and frolic until Ajax was seen coming around the driveway in the direction of the front entrance to the grounds.

"Ajax, what are you doing with those little monkeys? Where are you taking them?" cried Lily, hurrying down the veranda steps and running after him.

"Ober to Woodburn, where dey b'long, Miss Lily," he answered, pausing in his walk and turning toward her.

"Oh, I wish you wouldn't. I was most in hopes they'd let us keep them. They are such funny little fellows, I don't like to give them up."

"But I'se tole to take 'em dar, an' I'se got to do it," replied Ajax in a regretful tone. "I'll fetch 'em back hyar ef de Woodburn folks 'low me to."

"But they won't. They'll be sure to keep them if they're there," sobbed the little girl, tears rolling down her cheeks.

But even as she spoke, a hand was laid gently on her shoulder, and her father's voice said in kindest tones, "Don't cry, daughter dear. We must let the tee-tees go home to their owners, but you and Laurie shall have other pets in place of them. I have a pretty Maltese kitten bought for you and a fine dog for your brother. Come back to the veranda, and these new pets shall be brought out."

"Oh, papa, how nice! Thank you ever so much!" cried Lily, brushing away her tears and putting her hand in his to be led back to the veranda, where the new pets were speedily produced to the evident delight of the young owners and the admiration of their guests.

And when Ajax returned with Captain Raymond's kindly expressed thanks, Lily's grief seemed fully assuaged.

The older people, who had paused in their more important conversation to observe what was going on among the children, now resumed it, Grandma Elsie asking Walter of his engagements during the past winter. He replied that he had been busy with his studies, but that he had found some time for missionary work, especially on the Sabbath, among the poor and degraded, particularly foreigners of the lower class.

"And mother," he added, "I have quite decided that I want to go into the ministry. I want to be a missionary to the poor and needy, the ignorant and helpless."

"My dear son," she replied with emotion, "how glad I am to hear it! I want you to be a winner of souls, a helper of the helpless in this, your own land, or in some other—preferably this, because then you will be nearer to me and I can see you more often."

"Yes, mother," he added, "and I think I could hardly find a better field than among the mountains of Kentucky or Tennessee."

"No, I don't believe you could," said his grandfather approvingly. "Those mountaineers are our own people, and some are destitute as regard to both temporal and spiritual things and have a prior claim to that of those in heathen lands. Love for our land and nation should draw us strongly to their aid, even if we did not care for their eternal salvation."

Others in the little company gave expression to similar views and feelings, and they discussed ways and means of helping the work already going on among those mountaineers. There was a general expression of intention to do more for that corner of the Lord's vineyard than they had ever yet done.

"And by way of carrying out our intentions, suppose we take up a collection now," suggested Edward Travilla.

"I doubt if that would be our wisest course if we want to give liberally," remarked his sister Elsie. "For I presume no one has much in hand at this moment."

"So I dare say our motto just now would better be a lazy one, 'Not today, we'll do it tomorrow'," laughed Zoe.

"Yes. Let us appoint a collector for tomorrow," said her husband. "I propose Walter for the job. All in favor say 'aye.'" It was an invitation which all immediately accepted.

"I am quite willing," he said, "and shall include Woodburn folks and maybe some of the nearby relatives in my list of hoped-for and tried-for subscribers. I expect to come calling in good season tomorrow morning. So please all be ready for prompt compliance with my solicitation."

Then Mr. Dinsmore suggested that it might be well now to have the evening family devotions ere the young folks grew too weary and sleepy to enjoy a share in them. In response, all were called within doors, and the service held.

About the same time, similar services were going on at Woodburn, after which the Sunnyside folk bade goodnight and sought their own homes, Chester drawing Ray in his new coach and a servant doing a like service for baby Mary. Her devoted mother walked close by the side of the dainty little vehicle.

The next morning, Chester set off for his place of business at his usual hour, and just as he disappeared down the road, Lucilla, still standing upon the veranda, saw to her delight her father approaching from Woodburn.

"Oh, father," she cried, "I am so glad to see you this morning."

"Are you?" he said, coming up the steps and taking her in his arms for a tender caress. "Well, daughter dear, the joy is mutual. How is my little grandson this morning?"

"Well, I believe, father, but he is still asleep. Won't you come in and have a cup of coffee?"

He accepted the invitation, and they chatted together while she finished her breakfast, Chester's hurried departure having called her away from the table a trifle too soon.

The nurse brought Ray in, washed and dressed for the day, just as they finished their coffee.

"Give him to me," said the captain, and taking him in his arms, he carried him out onto the veranda, Lucilla following.

It was a warm morning, and they sat down there side by side.

"To his grandfather, he seems a lovely little darling," the captain said, caressing the child as he spoke. "Lucilla, my daughter, I hope you will prove a good, kind, patient, faithful mother, bringing him up in the nurture and admonition of the Lord."

"Oh, father," she replied in tones tremulous with emotion, "I want to do so, but—oh, you know what a bad natural temper I have. I very much fear that I shall not always be patient with him, even as dearly as I love him."

"Watch and pray, daughter dear. Ask the Lord daily, hourly for strength, grace, and wisdom according to your need. God is the hearer and answerer of prayer. He says, 'Call upon Me in the day of trouble. I will deliver thee and thou shalt glorify Me.' Trust in Him, and He will deliver you from the power of the tempter and your own evil nature."

"I will, father. I do," she said. "It helps and comforts me to know that you pray for me, especially remembering that gracious, precious promise of our Lord, 'If two of you shall agree, as touching anything that they shall ask, it shall be done for them of my Father which is in heaven.'"

"Yes, it is indeed a gracious, precious promise, and it can never fail," he said. "But now I must go, daughter. You and Eva come over to Woodburn again today as early as may suit your convenience," he added, putting the child into her arms and giving each a good-bye caress.

Shortly after breakfast at Ion that morning, Walter walked over to Fairview and called upon the Lelands for their contributions for the benefit of the Kentucky and Tennessee mountaineers. All, father and mother to youngest child, gave liberally in proportion to their ability.

"Oh, I am delighted!" exclaimed Walter. "I think I shall go on and present the cause to all the kith and kin in this neighborhood."

"Do," said his sister. "There won't be one who will not give according to his or her ability. And when through with this, brother dear, come here and pay us as long a visit as you can."

"Thank you, I think I shall, especially if you get mother to be here at the same time. I don't want to miss a minute of her society."

"Which you cannot love better than I do," returned his sister with a look that said more than her words. "She is decidedly fond of us both, and I think she will not refuse to accompany you here at my earnest request or to stay as long as you do."

"No, indeed. I am very sure she won't. I am going back now to Ion, and mother will go with me in the gig to drive around to the home of each of our relatives and near connections in this neighborhood and ask them to give what they can or would like to give to this good cause. We will take Woodburn last and get either Harold or the captain to put the money in the right shape—a check, I suppose—and mail it so that it will reach the proper spot as soon as possible."

With that, Walter bade good-bye and hastened to carry out his plans, which he, with his mother's help, did successfully. Everyone solicited by them gave liberally to the good cause, and the captain attended promptly to the dispatch of the funds.

CHAPTER TWENTIETH

THAT MAY DAY ended in a lovely evening warm enough to make outside air the most agreeable. So, directly after an early tea, the Woodburn family gathered upon the veranda, where they were presently joined by the Sunnyside folk, babies and all, who received the warmest of welcomes, though they had been absent from the older home but a few hours.

Naturally, the first topic of conversation related to that day's visit from Grandma Elsie and Walter and its main object—the appeal for help to the good word going on among the mountaineers of Kentucky and Tennessee.

"I am glad we were given the opportunity to help it," remarked the captain. "It has set me to thinking of the pioneers and early settlers of that section of our land, among them Daniel Boone and Simon Kenton."

"Oh, papa, please tell us about them!" exclaimed Elsie.

"Some time, daughter," he answered in his usual pleasant tones. "But the rest of this little company may not care to hear the old stories repeated just now."

At that, there was unanimous expression of desire to do so, and so he presently began.

"Simon Kenton's lifetime took in both our wars with England, as he was born in 1755 and lived until April of 1836. Virginia was his native state, but his father was Irish and his mother Scotch. They were poor, and Simon received but little education. At the age of sixteen, he had a fight with another young fellow named William Veach about a love affair. He thought he had killed Veach, so he fled over the Alleghenies. There he was called Simon Butler. He formed friendships with traders and hunters, among them Simon Girty."

"Girty—that cruel, cruel wretch!" cried Elsie. "How could anybody want to have him for a friend, papa?"

"He was a bad, cruel man," replied her father, "but perhaps he never had any good teaching. His father died, and his mother married again. Then they were all taken prisoner by the Indians, and his step-father was burned at the stake when Simon Girty was but five years old. It was three years before he was released, and I do not know if he ever had any education. Many cruel deeds are told of him, but he was really a good friend to Simon Kenton. Once, he saved him from being burned at the stake by the Indians.

"But to go back, Kenton was soon persuaded by a young man named Yager, who had been taken by some western Indians when a child and spent a good many years among them, to go with him to a land called by the Indians Kan-tuc-kee, which he described as a most delightful place.

"They two, with a third young man named Strader, set off in high spirits, expecting to find a paradise, but they wandered through the wilderness for weeks hoping to find the promised land without success. Then they tried hunting and trapping for nearly two years. But being discovered by the Indians, they had to abandon those hunting grounds and try elsewhere. To tell of it all would make too long a story.

"In 1778, Kenton joined Daniel Boone in his expedition against the Indian town on Paint Creek. On his return from that, he was sent to Colonel Bowman with two companions to make observations upon the Indian towns on Little Miami, the colonel considering the idea of an expedition against them. Kenton reached the spot in safety, and if he had attended only to what he was sent to do he might have succeeded well and been very useful to the settlers in Kentucky. But before leaving the towns, he stole a number of the Indians' horses.

"The Indians missed their horses early the next morning, found the trail of those who had taken them, and at once pursued after them. Kenton and his companions soon heard the cries of the Indians in their rear and knew they were being pursued. They obviously saw the necessity of riding for their lives, which they did, dashing through the woods at a furious rate, with the hue and cry of the Indians after them ringing in their ears. But suddenly and without warning, they came to an impenetrable swamp.

"There they paused a few moments, listening for the sounds of pursuit. Hearing none, they started on again, skirted the swamp for some distance, hoping to be able to cross it. Finding they could not, they dashed in a straight line for the Ohio River. For forty-eight hours, they continued their furious speed, halting only once or twice for a few minutes to eat a little, and they reached the Ohio in safety. But there they had to pause and consider what to do, for the river was high and rough and the jaded horses could not be induced to try to swim it. The men might yet have escaped if they had only abandoned the horses, but that Kenton could not make up his mind what to do. He and his companions consulted over the matter, and feeling sure that they were as much as twelve hours in advance of their Indians pursuers, they decided to conceal the horses in the nearby ravine and themselves in an adjoining wood. They hoped that by sunset the high wind would abate and the river become quiet enough for them to cross safely with the animals.

"But when the waited-for time came, the wind was higher and the water rougher than ever. Still they stayed where they were through the night. The next morning was mild, and they heard no sound of pursuing Indians, so they again tried to urge the horses over the river. But the animals seemed to remember its condition on the previous day and could not be induced to go into it at all.

"It was quite a drove of horses they had stolen, but now they found they must abandon all but the three they could mount. So that they did and started down the river with the intention to keep the Ohio and Indiana side until they should arrive opposite Louisville.

"But they had waited too long, and even now they were slow in carrying out their intention. They had not gone more than a hundred yards on their horses when they heard a loud halloo, coming apparently from the spot they had just left. They could not escape and were quickly surrounded by their pursuers. One of Kenton's companions was killed, and the other, effecting his escape while Kenton was being taken prisoner, fell victim to his love of horses."

"I suppose he deserved it, as he had stolen the horses," remarked Elsie.

"Yes," replied her father. "He had no more right to steal from the Indians than from white people, and his sin found him out."

"Did they kill him, papa?" asked Ned.

"No, they kicked and cuffed him as much as they cared to then made him lie down upon his back and stretch his arms to their full length, passed a stout stick across his chest, and fastened his wrists to each extremity of it by thongs of buffalo-hide. Then they drove stakes into the ground near his feet and fastened them in the same way. After that, they tied a halter around his neck and fastened it to a sapling growing near. Lastly, they passed a strong rope under his body and wound it several times around his arms at the elbows, so lashing them to the stick which lay across his chest and to which his wrists were fastened. All this was done in a manner that was peculiarly painful. He could not move at all, either feet, arms, or head, and he was kept in that position until the next morning. Then, as they wanted to go back to the spot from which they had come, they unfastened him, put him on the back of a wild, unbroken colt, one of those he had stolen, lashed him by the feet to it, and tied his hands behind him. And so he was driven into cruel captivity, a captivity which has been spoken of as being singular and remarkable in other respects as any in the whole history of Indian warfare upon this continent.

"Kenton refused with strange infatuation to adopt proper measures for his safety while he might have done so. With strange obstinacy he remained on the Ohio shore until flight became useless. He was often at one hour tantalized with a prospect of safety and the next plunged into the deepest despair. Eight times he had to run the gauntlet, three times he was tied to a stake and thought himself about to suffer a terrible death. Any sentence passed upon him by one council, whether to give him mercy or death, would presently be reversed by another. Whenever Providence raised up a friend in his favor, some enemy immediately followed, unexpectedly interposed and turned his glimpse of sunshine in deeper darkness than ever. For three weeks, he was in that manner seesawing between life and death."

"And did they kill him at last, papa?" asked Ned quietly.

"No," replied the captain. "An Indian agent of the name of Drewyer, who was anxious to gain intelligence for the British commander at Detroit in regard to the strength and condition of the settlements in Kentucky, got Kenton free from the Indians just as for the fourth time they were about to bind him to a stake and burn him. Drewyer did not get anything of importance out of Kenton, who was three weeks later sent a prisoner to Detroit, from which place he made his escape in about eight months. Then he went back to Kentucky. He was very brave—a valuable scout, a hardy woodsman, and a good Indian fighter. He performed many daring feats as the friend and companion of Daniel Boone, once saving his life in a conflict with the Indians."

"Had not Logan something to do with Kenton's rescue by that Canadian trader Drewyer?" asked Harold, who had been listening with interest to the captain's story.

"Yes," was the reply, "Logan, the Mingo chief. At Detroit, Kenton was held as a prisoner of war, and there he worked for the garrison at half pay until he was aided by a trader's wife to escape. That was in July of 1779. He commanded a battalion of Kentucky volunteers as a major under Anthony Wayne in 1793 and 1794. He became a brigadier-general of the Ohio militia in 1805, and he fought bravely at the battle of the Thames in 1813."

"I hope his country rewarded his great services as it ought," remarked Gracie in tones of inquiry.

"Ah!" replied her father, "I am sorry to say that in his old age, he was reduced to poverty, the immense tracts of land which he possessed being lost through the invasion of settlers and his ignorance of the law.

"In 1824, he went to Frankfort to petition the legislature of Kentucky to release the claim of the state upon some mountain land owned by him. He was in tattered garments, and his appearance excited ridicule, but on being recognized by General Thomas Fletcher, he was taken to the capitol, seated in the speaker's chair, and introduced to a large assembly as the second grand adventurer of the West. His lands were released and a pension of $240 was procured for him from Congress.

"He died near the spot where, fifty-eight years before, he had escaped death at the hands of the Indians. Kenton County, Kentucky, was named in his honor.

"Now let me read you a passage from a book I was examining the other day, in which there is an interesting account of Kenton's appearance and manner in his old age," said the captain. "It's in the library, and I shall be back with it in a moment."

Several of the younger ones in the company at once offered to do the errand for him, but thanking them and saying that he could find it more readily than they, he went in and soon returned with the book in his hand. He then read aloud, "'Kenton's form, even under the weight of seventy-nine years, is striking, and must have been a model of manly strength and agility. His eyes if blue are mild and yet penetrating in its glance. The forehead projects very much at the eyebrows, which are well defined, and then recedes, and is neither very high nor very broad. His hair, which in active life was light, is now quite gray. His nose is straight, and his mouth before he lost his teeth must have been expressive and handsome. I observed that he had yet one tooth, which, in connection with his character and manner of conversation, was continually reminding me of Leatherstocking. The whole face is remarkably expressive, not of turbulence or excitement, but rather of rumination and self-possession. Simplicity, frankness, honesty, and strict regard to truth appeared to be the prominent traits of his character. In giving an answer to a question which my friend asked him, I was particularly struck with his truthfulness and simplicity. The question was, whether the account of his life, given in the *Sketches of Western Adventure* was true or not. "Well, I'll tell you," said he, "not true. The book says that when Blackfish, the Injun warrior, asked me, when they had taken me prisoner, if Colonel Boone sent me to steal their horses, I said, 'No, sir.'" Here he looked indignant and rose from his chair. "I tell you I never said 'sir' to an Injun in my life. I scarcely ever say it to a white man." Here Mrs. Kenton, who was engaged in some domestic occupation at the table, turned round and remarked that when they were last in Kentucky someone gave her the book to read to her husband, and that when she came to that part he would not let her read any further. "And I tell you," continued he, "I was never tied to a stake in my life to be burned. They had me painted black when I saw Girty but not tied to a stake." We are inclined to think, notwithstanding this, that the statement in the *Sketches* of his being three times tied to the stake is correct, for the author of that interesting work had before him a manuscript account of the pioneer's life, which had been dictated by Mr. Kenton to a gentleman of Kentucky a number of years before, when he had no motive to exaggerate and his memory was comparatively unimpaired. But he is now beyond the reach of earthly toil, or trouble, or suffering. His old age was as exemplary as his youth and manhood had been active and useful. And though his last years were clouded by poverty, and his eyes closed in a miserable cabin to the light of life, yet shall he occupy a bright page in our border history and his name soon open to the light of fame.'"

A slight pause followed the conclusion of the captain's reading of the sketch of the life of Kenton, and then Gracie said earnestly, "Thank you, father, for giving us so extended an account of Kenton's life and services to our country. He deserved the kindly and grateful remembrance of his countrymen."

"So I think," said Harold, "and that he will never be forgotten. Poor fellow! I am sorry indeed that he was robbed of his lands and so spent his old age and died in poverty."

CHAPTER
TWENTY-FIRST

THE NEXT DAY was the Sabbath—the first since the return of the friends from Viamede. They attended, as usual, the morning services of the sanctuary, and in the afternoon, they gathered upon the veranda at Woodburn for the private, conversational study of some scriptural theme.

"What is to be our lesson for today, captain?" queried Mr. Lilburn when they had seated themselves, each with Bible in hand.

"I have thought of the sacrificial shedding of blood," was the reply. "Here in Hebrews 9:22, 'And almost all things are by the law purged with blood; and without shedding of blood is no remission.' The blood of sacrifices was typical of the atoning blood of Christ. Paul tells us, 'Neither by the blood of goats and calves, but by His own blood He entered in once into the holy place, having obtained eternal redemption for us . . . So Christ was offered to bear the sins of many.' Now, let us read in turn texts bearing upon this great subject. Violet, my dear, will you begin?"

"Yes," she replied. "The books of Matthew, Mark, and Luke each tell of Jesus' words in giving His disciples the cup of wine at His last supper on earth. He said to them, 'This is My blood of the new testament, which is shed for many for the remission of sins.'"

It was now Harold's turn, and he read: "'Then Jesus said unto them, "Verily, verily, I say unto you, except ye eat the flesh of the Son of man, and drink His blood, ye have no life in you. Whoso eateth my flesh, and drinketh my blood, hath eternal life; and I will raise him up at the last day. For my flesh is meat indeed, and my blood is drink indeed. He that eateth my flesh, and drinketh My blood, dwelleth in Me, and I in Him."'"

It was now Gracie's turn, and she read: "'Take heed, therefore, unto yourselves, and to all the flock, over the which the Holy Ghost hath made you overseers to feed the church of God, which He hath purchased with His own blood.'"

Then little Elsie read: "'Whom God hath set forth to be a propitiation through faith in His blood, to declare His righteousness for the remission of sins that are past, through the forbearance of God.'"

Then Ned: "'Much more, then, being now justified by His blood, we shall be saved from wrath through Him.'"

Grandma Elsie, sitting next, now read from Ephesians: "'But now in Christ Jesus ye who sometimes were far off are made nigh by the blood of Christ . . . In whom we have redemption through His blood, the forgiveness of sins, according to the riches of His grace.'"

Then Lucilla: "'Neither by the blood of goats and calves, but by His blood He entered in once into the holy place, having obtained eternal redemption for us. For if the blood of bulls and goats, and the ashes of an heifer sprinkling the unclean, sanctifieth to the purifying of the flesh: how much more shall the blood of Christ, who through the eternal Spirit offered Himself without spot to God, purge your conscience from dead works to serve the living God?'"

Then Chester read: "'Having, therefore, brethren, boldness to enter into the holiest by the blood of Jesus, by a new and living way, which He hath consecrated for us, through the veil, that is to say, His flesh . . . of how much sorer punishment, suppose ye, shall he be thought worthy, who hath trodden under foot the Son of God and hath counted the blood of the covenant, wherewith He has sanctified, an unholy thing, and hath done despite unto the Spirit of grace?'"

Evelyn, sitting next, then read: "'Unto Him that loved us and washed us from our sins in His own blood, and hath made us kings and priests unto God and His Father; to Him be glory and dominion for ever and ever.'"

Then Mrs. Annis Lilburn, sitting next, read: "'And they sung a new song, saying, "Thou art worthy to take the book and to open the seals thereof: for thou wast slain, and hast redeemed us to God by Thy blood out of every kindred and tongue and people and nation.'"'"

Walter sat next, and he read: "'These are they which came out of great tribulation, and have washed their robes, and made them white in the blood of the Lamb.'"

Then Mr. Lilburn, next and last, read: "'And they overcame him by the blood of the Lamb, and by the word of their testimony.' The one there spoken of as overcome is, as doubtless you know, Satan, spoken of in this chapter of Revelation as the accuser of our brethren, accusing them before God day and night. But by the blood of the Lamb of God, and only by that, could they or anyone overcome him."

"'Who his own self bare our sins in His own body on the tree, that we, being dead to sins, should live unto righteousness: by whose stripes ye were healed,'" quoted Grandma Elsie in moved tones. "Oh, how can we help loving Him with all our hearts and serving Him with all our powers?"

"'For Christ also hath once suffered for sins, the just for the unjust, that He might bring us to God, being put to death in the flesh, but quickened by the Spirit,'" quoted the captain. Then he added: "'The blood of Jesus Christ His son cleanseth us from all sin.'"

Lucilla followed: "'Herein is love, not that we loved God, but that He loved us, and sent His son to be the propitiation for our sins.'"

Evelyn followed Lulu: "'Ye know that He was manifested to take away our sins; and in

Him is no sin . . . He is the propitiation for our sins; and not for our's only, but also for the sins of the world.'"

"'And we have seen and do testify that the Father sent the Son to be the Savior of the world. Whosoever shall confess that Jesus is the Son of God, God dwelleth in him and he in God,'" quoted Violet with feeling. Then she started a hymn, in which all joined with fervor:

"Come, let us sing of Jesus,
While hearts and accents blend;
Come, let us sing of Jesus,
The sinner's only Friend;
His holy soul rejoices,
Amid the choirs above,
To hear our youthful voices
Exulting in His love.

"We love to sing of Jesus,
Who wept our path along;
We love to sing of Jesus,
The tempted and the strong;
None who besought His healing
He passed unheeded by,
And still retains His feeling
For us above the sky.

"We love to sing of Jesus,
Who died our souls to save;
We love to sing of Jesus,
Triumphant o'er the grave;
And in our hour of danger
We'll trust His love alone
Who once slept in a manger,
And now sits on the throne.

"Then let us sing of Jesus
While yet on earth we stay,
And hope to sing of Jesus
Throughout eternal day;
For those who here confess Him
He will in heaven confess,
And faithful hearts that bless Him
He will forever bless."

That hymn finished, Grandma Elsie started
another beautiful one, in which all joined:

"I love to tell the story
Of unseen things above,
Of Jesus and His glory,
Of Jesus and His love.
I love to tell the story,
Because I knew 'tis true;
It satisfies my longings
As nothing else can do.

Chorus:
"I love to tell the story,
'Twill be my theme in glory—
To tell the old, old story
Of Jesus and His love.

"I love to tell the story;
More wonderful it seems
Than all the golden fancies
Of all our golden dreams.
I love to tell the story,
It did so much for me;
And that is just the reason
I tell it now to thee.

"I love to tell the story—
'Tis pleasant to repeat
What seems, each time I tell it,

More wonderfully sweet;
I love to tell the story,
For some have never heard
The message of salvation
From God's own Holy Word.

"I love to tell the story
For those who know it best
Seen hungering and thirsting
To hear it like the rest;
And when, in scenes of glory
I sing the new, new song,
'Twill be the old, old story
That I have loved so long."

Several prayers followed the singing of the hymns, and then the meeting closed with the singing of the *Doxology*, in which all, old and young, took part.

CHAPTER
TWENTY-SECOND

THAT WEEK, THE FIRST after the return of the *Dolphin*, bringing the last installment of visitors from Viamede, was filled with family parties given in the daytime for the sake of the little ones, who in each case were quite as welcome as the older folk. But the weather was growing warm, and the doctors advised a speedy flitting in a more northerly direction.

"To do so speedily will be best for you all, especially my Gracie, Ned, and the little ones— Mary and Ray," said Dr. Harold Travilla, addressing the usual family party gathered for the evening upon the veranda at Woodburn.

"So I think," said the captain. "And as on like occasions in the past, the *Dolphin* is at the service of you all. She can be made fully ready in a day."

"And Crag Cottage will be ready and glad to accommodate you all as soon as the *Dolphin* can carry you there," added Evelyn in pleasant, playful tones.

"Oh, thank you, Eva," cried several voices. Lucilla added, "There is no place I should prefer to that." Then turning to her husband, "You can go, too. Can't you, Chester?"

"Perhaps for a brief sojourn. Then I will leave my wife and son there for a longer time, coming for them when fall weather shall have made it safe for them to come home again," he replied in cheerful tones. Then turning to Dr. Harold, "I hope," he added, "that you are intending to spend the summer there, keeping guard over our family treasures committed to your care?"

"I have planned upon doing so, providing Cousin Arthur and my brother Herbert will undertake the care of all our patients in this neighborhood, of which I have no doubt," was the ready reply. "Then I must take charge in the fall, giving them a vacation in their turn."

"Yes, I am very sure you will do right and generously by them," remarked Gracie, giving him a look of love and confidence.

"Oh, I am glad to think of being on our good *Dolphin* again and then at dear, sweet Crag Cottage," cried Ned, clapping his hands in delight. "Oh, papa, can't we have a voyage out in the ocean, too?"

"Perhaps so," said his father. "I see nothing to prevent, if all my passengers desire it. However, we can decide that question after going aboard the yacht."

"Yes, and I feel pretty sure we will all be in favor of a little trip far enough toward the east side of the ocean to be at least for a few hours out of sight of land on this side," laughed Lucilla.

"And how soon shall we start?" asked Chester.

"The yacht can be ready by the day after tomorrow," said the captain. "If all the passengers are ready by then, we will start in the evening of that day."

Violet, Evelyn, and Lucilla all replied at once that they could be ready almost at a moment's notice, having for weeks past been looking forward to this flitting and preparing for it.

"And, father," added Evelyn, "I should like to have Cousins Ronald and Annis Lilburn as my guests for the summer. Can you not invite them now through the telephone and ask how soon they can be ready, if willing to go?"

"I can," he replied in a pleased tone and went at once to the instrument.

Their answer was that they would be delighted to go and would be ready by the time mentioned for the starting of the vessel.

Captain Raymond then telephoned to Ion, told of the proposed starting of the *Dolphin* for a northern trip to end at Crag Cottage on the Hudson, and gave a warm invitation from Evelyn to Grandma Elsie and Walter to join the party and be her guests for the summer, if they should care to stay so long.

A gratified acceptance with an assurance that they would be ready in good season came in reply, and all the Woodburn company were quite jubilant over the prospect of the pleasant trip and the enjoyable summer at Crag Cottage likely to follow.

Captain Raymond kept his promise to have the *Dolphin* ready in due time, and all the passengers were aboard her when the anchor was lifted early in the evening of the appointed day. The weather was fine, and they found the deck a delightful place for the promenading or sitting at ease on the comfortable seats provided. There was much cheerful chat, sometimes mirthful, sometimes serious. There were jests and badinage, fun and frolic, especially among the children with Cousin Ronald to help it on, and there was music—first songs, afterward hymns of praise, repetitions of passages of Scripture, and prayers of thankfulness and petitions for God's protecting care. Then the little ones were sent to their nests for the night, and somewhat later the older ones retired to theirs.

Lucilla's idea of an eastward trip until out of sight of land was carried out to her satisfaction and amusement. Then the *Dolphin* turned, passed through Long Island Sound and up the Hudson River to Crag Cottage, which they reached in safety and all in good health.

There, as always before, they had a pleasant, restful time often enlivened by the fun Cousin Ronald's talent could make. After a while of varied trips here and there, Chester returned home with the understanding that he would probably be with them again before the season was over. He was missed, but with Mr. Lilburn, Captain Raymond, Dr. Harold, and Walter Travilla still left, the ladies and children were not without protectors and helpers of the stronger sex in their midst.

In a few days, a glad surprise was given them all, Evelyn in especial, by the unexpected arrival of Max. He had obtained a furlough and could be with them for some weeks.

"Now I think with two ventriloquists here, we shall have some fun," exclaimed Ned shortly after his brother's arrival.

"Ah, Ned, Ned, is that all you care about in seeing your only brother?" queried Max in tones of heartfelt disappointment and an expression of deep despondency.

"Oh, no, no, indeed!" cried Ned. "I'm ever so glad to have you here, Maxie, if you never do any ventriloquism at all. Please believe me."

"Well, I suppose I must, since I know you have been trained up to speak the truth," returned Max, brightening a little. "I hope the company of your only brother may afford you some slight enjoyment, even should there be no practice of ventriloquism during my visit."

"Yes, brother, you may be sure of it," replied Ned, striving to suppress a slight sigh.

"Your brother must be allowed an enjoyable time with his wife, little daughter, and new little nephew before we trouble him to attend to anything else," remarked Violet in an amused tone.

"In the meantime the rest of us can, perhaps, be depended upon to entertain your young laddie, Cousin Violet," said Mr. Lilburn with a kindly, amused look at Ned.

"I see that, as usual, you have the *Dolphin* lying here at your dock, father," said Max. "I suppose that you all take occasional trips in her."

"Yes, son, and I think you will not object to accompanying us in that. Will you?"

"Oh, no, sir. No, indeed. I shall be very glad to do so, as babies and all can be made quite as comfortable there as anywhere on land."

"By the way," said Dr. Harold, "a lady patient was telling me the other day of a visit she had paid to the village of Catskill. She had become interested in it because of having seen Joseph Jefferson playing 'Rip Van Winkle,' and that has given me a desire to see the place."

"So you shall," said the captain. "The *Dolphin* can readily be persuaded to make that trip, and I presume none of our party would object to going there in her."

He sent a smiling glance around as he spoke, and it was responded to by wide smiles and exclamations of pleasure in the prospect.

"I don't know anything about Rip Van Winkle," said Elsie, turning toward her father. "Is it a story, papa, and will you tell me about it?"

"Yes, daughter," he replied. "It is a story and only a story—not fact at all. But it seems so real as played by Jefferson that very many people were and are greatly interested in it. Rip Van Winkle is represented as an ignorant, good-natured man, who was made and kept poor by his love of liquor, which so soured his wife against him that she drove him out of the house. Once, it was at night and in a terrible thunderstorm. He goes into a steep and rocky clove in the Catskill Mountains and meets some queer, silent people, who gave him drinks of liquor that put him to sleep, and he does not wake up again for twenty years. In that time, he had changed from a comparatively young man to a feeble, old one with white hair and a long, white beard. In the meantime, his wife, thinking him dead, had married the man—Derrick by name—who had stolen his house and land. She had done it in order to keep herself and little daughter from starvation. He was now trying to force little Meenie, Rip's daughter, to marry his nephew, Cookles, though she did not want him, as she loved another, young Hendrick, who was her playmate when they were children. Hendrick is now a sailor and away on his vessel—has been gone for five years—but now he comes back just in time to put a stop to the mischief Derrick and his nephew, Cookles, are trying to do to Meenie and Gretchen in order to get full possession of the house and land. He and Rip are able to prove that those, the house and land, are not his and never were.

"So the story ends well. The scamps are at last defeated, and the rightful owners are happy in regaining the property and being restored to each other," concluded the captain.

"Thank you, papa," said Elsie. "That was a very nice story, indeed, because it ended better than I would have expected."

"And wouldn't you like to see the place where all this is said to have happened?" asked Dr. Harold of little Elsie.

"Yes, indeed," she answered. After a little more chat on the subject, it was decided that they would visit the village of Catskill the next day and see the very spot where all these strange events were supposed to have taken place.

"The scenery about there is said to be very fine. Is it not?" asked Mr. Lilburn.

"It is," replied Captain Raymond. "I think we who are strong enough to climb steep ascents will be well repaid for the effort. Our best plan will be to leave the yacht for a hotel, for in order to see all that is worth seeing, we must spend some days in the vicinity."

"Yes," said Dr. Harold, "and the ladies and babies and our not very strong little Ned will need to stay in the village while we stronger ones climb about the cliffs."

"I think you are right in that," assented his mother. "By the way," she continued, "do you think, gentlemen, that it was quite correct for an author of the play to bring in Hudson and some of his men as taking part in causing Rip's long nap? From the accounts given of his life and death, it would seem that he was set adrift by his sailors considerably more to the north and perished in the sea."

"That is so, mother," returned the captain. "It is all about as true as the story of Rip's long nap."

"That couldn't be true," remarked Elsie wisely, "for nobody could live half as long as that without eating anything. Could they, Uncle Harold?"

"No, certainly not," replied her uncle, smiling at the very idea. "No one but a very ignorant person could be made to believe the story is true."

"Still, we can enjoy looking at the scenes of the supposed occurrences," remarked Captain Raymond. "Shall we go tomorrow?"

Everyone seemed in favor of that proposition, and the next morning, the weather being favorable and the yacht in excellent condition, they started upon their trip shortly after breakfast.

Comfortable accommodations were found in the hotel at Catskill, and the ladies seemed well satisfied with what they could see and enjoy in going about the valley while the stronger members of the party should climb the steep cliffs and explore all the places where Rip was said to have wandered—especially the spot where his very long sleep was supposed to have been taken.

The beautiful scenery of that region was greatly enjoyed by all, male and female, old and young. So all agreed in prolonging their visit to a stay of several days. Then they boarded the yacht and started for their Crag Cottage home again.

Max was very fond of his baby daughter, and when they were all comfortably established aboard the yacht, he took her in his arms. As he did so, he was startled for an instant by a joyous exclamation that seemed to come from her very lips, "Oh, papa, I love you and am so glad you are here with mamma and me again."

Glancing at Cousin Ronald, Max laughed and replied, "Are you, daughter? Well, I hope the time will never come when you will be other than very glad to see your father."

"Ah, that's the first talking she's done in quite a while," laughed her mother.

"Oh, was it you who made her do it, Max?" asked Ned excitedly.

"No," replied Max. "I was as much surprised at the moment as anybody else. But isn't it natural that the joy of seeing her long absent father should loosen her tongue?"

"I guess it is more natural that Cousin Ronald should do it," laughed Ned. "He could, I know, and I suspect that he did."

"Do you plead guilty, Cousin Ronald?" queried Evelyn, giving him a look of amusement.

"Well, now, you should not be too curious, Cousin Eva," was the non-committal reply.

"Is she too curious?" asked Ned. "Don't you think, Cousin Ronald, that's it's all right for her to want to know what has made little Mary talk so well tonight?"

"Of course it is," little Mary seemed to say. "And I hope to talk a good deal while my papa is with us."

"Yes, I hope you will," said Ned. "I think he'll help you about it. Don't you wish you'd been climbing those mountains along with him?"

"No, Uncle Ned. It was nicer to be with mamma in the village."

Ned laughed at that, and turning to the other baby, he asked, "How was it with you, Ray? Didn't you want to go along with the big folks?"

"No. You ain't one of the big folks. Are you?" Ray seemed to reply. Ned colored, as there was a general laugh from those present.

"A good deal bigger and older than you are," was his rather ungracious rejoinder.

"Please, don't be vexed with my baby boy, little brother," said Lucilla. "You know he didn't say that himself. Somebody put the words into his mouth, or, to speak more liberally, caused them to seem to come from his tongue. He does not know how to talk at all."

"Oh, yes, I know, and I'm not vexed with him now," said Ned. "I oughtn't be, as I'm his uncle and want him to be fond of me. I hope he will be when he's old enough to know about such things, Lu."

"Yes, Ned, you may be sure he will," said Max. "You and I are going to try to be such nice, good uncles that he will be proud to own us as such."

"And I shall try to be such a grandfather that he and baby Mary will be proud to own me as theirs," said the captain.

"It will be strange, indeed, if they are not, father," said Lucilla.

"Yes, indeed! I am very proud of being your daughter, papa, as I think the others are," said

Gracie. "I am sure Max and Ned are proud of being your sons."

"Indeed, we are," said Max.

"I know I am," laughed Ned. "So now I guess we are all pleased with each other and are going home to Crag Cottage quite happy."

Everybody laughed at that, and all reached their temporary home in excellent spirits. It was a lovely and enjoyable one, situated as it was on a charming part of Hudson River's western bank. The house was comfortable and convenient, and the grounds were tastefully laid out and kept in excellent order. Max and Eva had reason to be proud of their country seat. They and most of their guests remained there for some weeks until Max's furlough expired and fall weather rendered the return to their warmer southern homes desirable. And the homeward journey in the *Dolphin* was a most agreeable winding up of their summer trip to the North.

The End

*Invite Little Elsie Dinsmore™ Doll
Over to Play!*

Breezy Point Treasures' Elsie Dinsmore™ Doll
brings Martha Finley's character to life in this
collectible eighteen-inch all-vinyl play doll
produced in conjunction with
Lloyd Middleton Dolls.

The Elsie Dinsmore™ Doll comes complete
with authentic Antebellum clothing and a
miniature Bible. This series of books emphasizes
traditional family values so your and your child's
character will be enriched as have
millions since the 1800s.

Doll available from:

Breezy Point Treasures, Inc.
124 Kingsland Road
Hayneville, GA 31036 USA

Call for details on ordering:

1-888-487-3777

or visit our website at

www.elsiedinsmore.com

If You Enjoyed
THE ORIGINAL
ELSIE CLASSICS
You May Want to Read
THE ORIGINAL
MILDRED CLASSICS

BEFORE Martha Finley finished the first six titles of The Elsie Books in 1876, she began a new series based on the Dinsmores' Midwestern relatives, the Keiths. Introducing Mildred Keith, the family's sixteen-year-old daughter, Martha Finley wove the characters of the two series together to fill in some of the gaps in the plot lines of her early Elsie stories and to provide further depth to her characters and their relationships with one another. In this way she enriched the Elsie stories that have thrilled girls for more than 130 years. The seven volumes in The Original Mildred Classics, all priced at $5.95 each, include:

Book 1
MILDRED KEITH
ISBN: 1-58182-227-8

Book 2
MILDRED AT ROSELANDS
ISBN: 1-58182-228-6

Book 3
MILDRED AND ELSIE
ISBN: 1-58182-229-4

Book 4
MILDRED'S MARRIED LIFE
ISBN: 1-58182-230-8

Book 5
MILDRED AT HOME
ISBN: 1-58182-231-6

Book 6
MILDRED'S BOYS AND GIRLS
ISBN: 1-58182-232-4

Book 7
MILDRED'S NEW DAUGHTER
ISBN: 1-58182-233-2